A
MOMENT of
SILENCE

A
MOMENT of
SILENCE

Aubrey Jones

THOMAS NELSON PUBLISHERS
Nashville • Atlanta • London • Vancouver

Published in Nashville, Tennessee, by Thomas Nelson, Inc., Publishers, and distributed in Canada by Word Communications, Ltd., Richmond, British Columbia.

Scripture references used in character dialog are paraphrased by the author.

The lyrics to "Wedding Song (There Is Love)" appearing on pages 194-195 are used by permission. Copyright © 1971 PUBLIC DOMAIN FOUNDATION, INC., All Rights Reserved.

Library of Congress Cataloging-in-Publication Data

Jones, Aubrey, 1941-
   A moment of silence / Aubrey Jones.
     p.   cm.
   ISBN 0-7852-7970-9
   1. High school teachers—United States—Fiction. 2. Prayer in the public schools—Fiction. I. Title.
PS3560.04575M66 1995
813'.54—dc20   94-46866
                                                  CIP

 **DEDICATION**

To Laura and Leane, who will never know the joy they
have given, unless they have children like themselves.

"A general dissolution of principles and manners will more surely overthrow the liberties of America than the whole force of the common enemy. While the people are virtuous they cannot be subdued: but when once they lose their virtue they will be ready to surrender their liberties to the first external or internal invader."

Samuel Adams (1722-1803)
Organizer of the Boston Tea Party
Signer of the Declaration of Independence
U. S. Congressman
Governor of Massachusetts

The fifth grader was small for his age and known as a troublemaker. As he stood up before the class, his mouth narrowed into a line of resignation drawn between the parentheses of his puffed out cheeks. Blinking twice, he began, "Last Saturday morning my dad took me fishing." The memory must have calmed him because he came close to grinning, took a deep, audible breath, and went on. "Dad was fixing breakfast, so I went outside. It was dark, but the sun was getting ready to come up. I looked up at a star and watched it twinkle. Then I thought how it would be if I was standing far, far away and the star was really the earth, and I was a long ways away. I thought, everything I know is there. I don't know nothing here." The boy shrugged. "Well—that's all."

The teacher checked a square in his grade book, took his reading glasses off, and tapped one of his bottom teeth with an earpiece. *My life,* he thought. "Next," he said, not moving his lips because the glasses still rested there. He checked more squares, listening and saying, "Next," until the bell rang for recess. When the room had clattered empty, he continued sitting in the too-small desk in the corner at the rear of the room, looking at the cardboard picture of George Washington's face fastened over the chalkboard at the front. *Real George. Wonder who first said that? Probably Martha. Was he real or just cardboard?* Another birthday was coming up Wednesday for the father of this country. And today, another birthday for Robert Farr, the father of his children, and a teacher—his forty-fourth.

Today's date, February 20, 1989, was written on the board beneath George's picture. Two hundred fifty-seven years ago, the father of his country, having been conceived in liberty and dedicated to the proposition that all men were created . . .

"Mr. Farr," said a distant woman's voice from just outside the door at the front of the room.

"Back here."

The elderly teacher walked in with a subdued version of her frequent greeting, "How's Jefferson Elementary's best male teacher?"

"Stuck. How do you get out of one of these things?" he asked, pointing down at the desk.

"You learn not to get in in the first place."

"The first place? That was a long time ago. I could fit in it then."

Eunice Phillips started toward him but stopped. Composure all but fled from her face, leaving it older and more deeply lined. Holding the desk down, he stood. "What's wrong?" he asked.

"Robert—" Her practiced voice was steady, but the woman was crying.

He walked toward her, and her eyes seemed to find hope in his movement. "What is it, Eunice?"

"Natasha James—she was a sixth grade student in Judy Bowen's class—"

"Yes, I know Natasha."

"Natasha is dead. She was stabbed in the throat last night by Willa Denson."

"*Our* Willa Denson?"

"Yes, they were arguing over a boy and a can of beer."

Robert Farr turned and gazed out the windows across the room. The smell of children outside running or standing around talking in blurry patches of color and overcast lingered . . . not a bad odor, not a good one either. Only when he thought about it did the odor remind him of baths not taken. He remembered he should look at Eunice so he wouldn't seem rude. "How many does Natasha make?"

The aged face beholding him was like a December tree with all its leaves fallen and blown away, dark lines starkly etched under gray with a scent—neither good nor bad—of earthiness. "Four, including the suicides."

He lifted his eyes from her to George. "I'm sorry. I know how many."

"I know."

He felt a need to cry. But not this time; it would just embarrass him afterward. Besides, Connelly might pop in as she had before and thank him for doing his part for gender equality.

"Ms. Mayhew-Barr left a message for you," Eunice said,

looking away. "She wants you to make an announcement about Natasha over the intercom. Don't mention Willa. Just say Natasha died. Then she wants you to observe a moment of silence."

"Me? Why?"

"I think you know."

"She's the principal. Shouldn't she do that?"

"She's not here. The police wanted a statement from her, so she went to the station."

Robert pondered Eunice's face. They both knew why Mayhew-Barr asked him. It was his faith. "Okay."

"At the end of the time, just say, 'Thank you.'"

"Sure, no problem."

The woman left the room to be filled with silence while he stood and watched. Everything seemed to be changing before his eyes, yet the stillness overpowered thinking or knowing, and even feeling was falling away like leaves on a tree on some distant world too far away to know. Or some face or tree somewhere.

Time passed, and he looked out the window feeling recess about to end and with it another season of innocence for the children and for himself and for the world sitting there on the desk tilted at just the right angle to the sun that came through the windows once on a green day long ago. Somewhere down the hall a stick-figure girl in a green triangle with broomlike arms and hands grins a red smiley to other little smiley sticks with a bubble-drawn house and black crayon smoke stabbing from the chimney. Natasha had drawn herself in green.

Just say, "Thank you."

A bell rang, jangling time back into place with a click felt but not heard. Yet time didn't fit anymore, anymore than he fit in the too-small desk in the back or the just-right desk at the front. Anymore? *That's all—for now,* Mayhew-Barr had said. But it wasn't.

Stamping feet, voices, and chaos were spilling down the tiled halls. "Quietly!" a woman's young voice cried out with all the authority of bygone days. "Quietly!" But the chaos came on unabated. In his mind, Robert saw the loudest kids buffooning their way to his door, then his senses crescendoed as they came in as boisterously as pirates back from the sea with their plunder. Smells of fresh air and body odor swirled around the laughter, the pushing, and the wire spiral of the grade book between his fingers almost hurting. A boy tried to wrestle with a girl, but the match quickly ended when Robert took a step toward them.

"Is it true Natasha James got slashed?" a girl asked loudly as he continued to the front of the room.

"Sure, stupid!" said another. "Bad Willa hit the bingo spot! Natash is *noo-moe!*"

"Noo-moe! Noo-moe!" chanted a boy trying to start a rap, "No—"

Robert turned and faced the class. "That's enough! Now—" His next words were efficiently quiet. "Sit down."

They did, and he stood looking in turn at each face in the class. He saw that not every child—perhaps none of them—took the happening lightly. "Natasha James is dead," he said. "A human life is gone from this world—and each of us, whether we know it or not, will be a little sadder for the rest of our lives because she's gone."

The new aide was standing in the doorway. When he looked at her, she said, "Mr. Farr, you're needed in the office. I'll stay here if you want to go now."

"Thank you." He gave the class a look of instruction to keep the lid on while he was gone, laid his reading glasses on the desk, and walked past her into the hall. Her perfume would have told him that she was new even if he had not known. New teachers and aides sloshed it on, but eventually they either gave up the perfume, or just gave up. This aide would probably stay, he thought, because the fragrance reminded him of Paula.

Deserted, the hallway featured valentines, hearts, cherry trees, and Georges attached to bulletin boards, doors, and display cases. As he trudged from the last room on the longest wing of the school, Robert reviewed the two factors that he felt sure had led to this walk. First, according to Ms. Mayhew-Barr, the principal, he had made an "inappropriate religious comment" upon being introduced to the faculty when he had come three years before. She had promptly canceled his assignment as general science teacher and given him the most disruptive group of students in the school, not learning-disabled kids, but kids he had come to know as the abused, confused, and educationally unenthused.

The second factor was that Robert Farr had not quit. Nor had he argued; he just said, "Fine," and saw his response cloud Mayhew-Barr's face even further. That cloud had apparently rained animosity for him throughout the faculty and staff because the harassment had started immediately.

Slowing his walk, he took a deep breath, squared his

shoulders, and wondered if he would not have been better off to have quit that day, or at least protested—he could have won; he had a contract. But no, Robert Farr had not quit or protested, and he didn't retaliate against the harassment because having made the statement with his mouth, he was determined to make the same statement every day, at least with his life. It was like—well, life and death. And what the boy—also named Robert—had said about the world and not knowing rang a bell somewhere, but after all, didn't bells run his life? Bells and the people who rang them—Robert hesitated at the office door, then turned the knob and went in.

"Good morning," he said to two secretaries and an aide. The aide, Stacy Robertson, smiled and nodded; the secretaries turned away. Robert walked around the end of the counter and over to the intercom station on a table against the far wall. He was ready to press the *All Call* button when someone cleared her throat behind him.

"Farr—"

He turned to the secretary, who said through a broad grin, "The *boss* said—" She dangled a slip of paper between a thumb and forefinger in front of his face. "Read this announcement *exactly* as it's written."

He took the paper, and she flounced away. As he silently read the announcement, his breathing quickened in anger over the intolerance of those who preached tolerance so loudly. Thoughts of quitting then and there jammed his brain; but that would jeopardize Michael and Penny's welfare, and he saw himself struggling to explain to them why he had given up. Besides, he had a class waiting for him stuck in the back of the far wing. His finger went to the *All Call* button and pushed. The announcement would be made anyhow, and if he quit because of it, it would probably be framed and displayed in the teachers' lounge.

"Attention—all faculty—" he heard his voice reverberating down the halls as he read. "A seminar entitled 'The Foundation of Scientific Evolution for Current Educational Methodology' will be offered at State University, Saturday, March 4, from 9:00 A.M. until 3:00 P.M. with an hour off for lunch. This seminar will take place in Kaiser Hall and will focus on countering attacks upon evolution by the uninformed. All faculty members are urged to attend."

Robert paused with the button still depressed. He closed his eyes and opened them, looked at the wall, then down at the array of push-buttons on the console. "Also—" The word rolled like thunder down the halls and over the paper trees and hearts. It filled space and erased meaning from a drawing of dead sticks in green. Everyone in the school already knew; the words would be only polite formality.

"Natasha James, a student in Ms. Bowen's sixth grade class, died yesterday. Let us observe a moment of silence in her memory." Robert noted the position of the second hand on his watch as Natasha's minute began ticking away and fragments of her life as he knew her came to mind. She came running again to tell him that a bird had fallen from its nest in the cedar tree at the rear of the playground. He watched her put it back and remembered that she had cried the next day when it was on the ground again—dead. He watched her walking down the silent hall until she was gone, and he prayed silently for her family, whoever they were, whoever knew the girl and loved her. Then Natasha's minute was gone. "Amen," Robert said quietly, without thinking, then added, "Thank you." He released the button and straightened up.

Stacy Robinson was standing at the counter with a sad look on her face. She seemed anxiously preoccupied until a question burst forth. "You never had Natasha in your class, did you, Mr. Farr?"

"No," he replied, placing the announcement about the seminar on the counter. "I didn't know her very well. Did you?"

"No." The young woman seemed to want to say more while busying herself with a stack of papers. "No, I only knew her by sight."

One of the secretaries walked over to stand at the end of the counter where Robert would have to pass as he left. She put a hand on the counter and eyed him coldly. "Ms. Mayhew-Barr is going to know about what you've done here today!" she stated sharply.

"What have I done?"

"You made a religious statement! You said, 'Amen'! There can be no formal prayers . . ."

"I didn't offer a formal prayer, I simply . . ."

"You prayed! That word is well known as part of the nomenclature of a particular narrow-minded religious viewpoint. You violated the law!"

"Ms. Dunstal," Robert replied quietly, "the word simply means 'so be it.'"

"What language does it come from?"

"I don't know. Hebrew or Greek, I suppose."

"What language was the Bible written in?"

"Hebrew and Greek."

"See! You sought to impose your beliefs upon the entire student body and all the faculty of this school!"

"So—*this* was one of the reasons *I* was asked to come in and observe the minute of silence—"

Stacy's eyes widened slightly as she gave him a hint of a nod.

"Mr. Farr," said the secretary, "are you so paranoid as to suggest that there's a conspiracy against you?"

"I suggest," he replied, "that I have a job to do. My class is waiting, and I need to get back."

Dunstal stepped back and gave a wave of her arm toward the door. "By all means, go back to your job, Mr. Farr. Because I don't think you're going to have one in this school much longer!"

"Well, as long as I have one, I intend to do it! Now, if you'll excuse me—" Robert walked between the secretary and the counter and left the office, closing the door softly behind him.

Halfway to his room, he passed the open door of Ms. Connelly's class. "Just a minute," came her voice from behind him. He stopped and turned around to see her coming toward him with something like a smile on her face. The expression evaporated when she stopped a few inches away from him and said, "You prayed. You violated the rights of every person in this school. You're going to pay for that!" The woman spun on her heels and went back into the classroom, leaving Robert wishing he had held his breath against the stink of her smoker's breath.

He turned back toward his classroom, but he didn't walk. He just closed his eyes and stood there clenching and unclenching his fists, trying to think why he shouldn't smash one through the glass of the display case a few feet away. Why he shouldn't leave a trail of *his* blood down the hall as policemen dragged him away again screaming for Paula. Why he shouldn't . . . Why he shouldn't . . . His heart was beating why he shouldn't in his ears. Why he shouldn't . . .

Last Saturday morning my dad took me fishing. . . . Then I thought how it would be if I was standing far, far away . . . It was Paula's blood . . . *Why I shouldn't. Far, far away* . . . her eyes closed one last time. A drunk, and driving again. *Hold on,* she said. She said, *Robert—hold on—for the children.* Then the night was inverted by his scream. *Paula!*

Robert Farr opened his eyes to find himself standing alone in the deserted hall, feeling the unreality of glaring headlights, crackling police radios, and flashing blue lights.

The woman's dead, said a voice numbed by glaring lights.

The headlights veered head-on. Robert slammed the breaks, jerking left. Broadside. Paula's side. He closed his eyes and laid his head back as far as he could against the nightmare of tires and glass. Paula's side. He had done the best he could, the police said. It was instinct. The doctors said the same. Instinct. Five years of living with the memory of an instinct.

Her face wasn't even scratched. She just whispered, *Hold on. Robert—hold on—for the children.* Then Paula had closed her eyes and was gone. *For the children.* It wasn't just Michael and Penny; it was all the children they—now he—would ever teach. They had both made commitments, then Paula was gone.

All these things faded quickly, and he pressed his mouth into the tolerance he had found for himself after such times and began to walk slowly. His rage and Connelly—everything dropped into some unknowably deep ocean that came from somewhere under the tolerance. Tolerance, his footsteps, and the converging lines of the hall seemed to echo in tones of a Saturday morning fishing trip. *Everything I know is there. I don't know nothing here.* He shrugged. *Well— that's all.*

Robert stopped at the last display window and looked through and into the glass. Valentines, pinned up and scattered like splotches of . . . Valentines. His image stood alone in the glass. He actually smiled and surprised himself a little, inexplicably remembering their wedding picture: a tuxedoed guy with dark hair and a beautiful blonde in white. Just like the figures on top of the cake, people said.

He walked the last few feet to the door of the classroom and stood there, thankful for the responsibility he felt returning like a long awaited tide. Every child in the room was bent over his or her desk working pencils back and forth and looking seriously determined. A few glanced up at him but went back to work as if they had seen nothing. The aide tiptoed to him and whispered, "I have them working on a puzzle. Could we talk for just a minute in the hall?"

He looked around the room at the bent forms and heard the scratching pencils. "Well—I guess so." Robert moved back into the hall several feet from the door.

The young woman came out, smiled, and said, "I'm Beatrice Bertram."

"I know. I'm Robert Farr. How did you cram so much quiet into that room?"

"I put a simple puzzle on the chalkboard and told them if anyone in the class could solve it, you would take them all out to eat at an expensive restaurant!"

"You what?!"

"Don't worry," said Beatrice, obviously enjoying herself, "the puzzle has no solution!"

"What is it?"

"An oblong divided into three parts, two boxes above, one below. The object is to draw an unbroken, connecting line through the walls of every part without going through a wall more than once or crossing the drawn line at all."

Robert groaned. "There *is* a solution! If you go *along* a line . . ."

She grinned. "This time, there's no going along! I ruled that out."

He glanced down and exhaled. "Good!"

"There are a lot of questions—" She waited until he had lifted his eyes to hers before continuing. "—that have no answer that we can know in this world." Beatrice was meeting his surprised gaze with a steadiness that was unsettling. "Isn't that right, Mr. Farr?"

Robert looked away, his eyes going to the wall display case he had almost smashed, and he felt, just a little, like a schoolboy hailed into the hall by his teacher. He savored the thought or feeling, or whatever it was, for a moment because somehow it was comforting and because he was trying hard to forget her perfume. She was an aide, not a teacher, and she was at least twenty years younger than he, and—he looked at her waiting face for a not-uncomfortable time; after all, *he* was a teacher. Finally, he said, "What do you mean?"

"I'm a Christian, too, Mr. Farr. And I thought you must be having a rough time of it right now." She moved back slightly as her brown eyes waited.

"I see. Well, I guess that's no secret."

"And I thought you might need a friend." She looked down the hall.

"Well—" He glanced at the door of the classroom. "You thought right."

"What about . . ." Beatrice hesitated, bringing her eyes back and smiling, possibly at her words before she said them. "Lunch today?"

"Lunch?"

"Yes. You know, in the cafeteria—"

Robert allowed a smile. "I know. Sure, I guess so."

Her jaw moved thoughtfully before she spoke. "I told your class that if they couldn't solve the puzzle, they would owe *you* a meal."

"In an expensive restaurant?"

She laughed. "No, in the cafeteria."

"Thanks," he said, trying to sound serious and failing. He paused and said it again, this time seriously, "Thanks."

"See you at the Café de Jeffersônne," Beatrice said over her shoulder as she turned to go.

"Fine." He felt the word as he said it like breathing a deep breath of fresh air. Robert fastened his eyes on the doorway to the classroom and hurried toward it. He went in and said, "Well, someone tell me, has anything been solved?"

The puzzle had not been solved, and when the lunch bell rang, Robert stood at the door to make sure all paper and pencils were left in the room. Their papers, which were supposed to have been tests on George Washington, had come in with the familiar patterns of boxes and broken, amoeba-shaped lines in the margins. Arguments and discussions about the possibility of solving the puzzle occurred among the children on the way to the cafeteria, and in class there had been outbursts of "I got it!" and replies of "Dummy!" when the solution was proved wrong. Far from being bothered by this disruption of his lesson plans, Robert had taken advantage of the opportunity to lead the class in discussions of success and failure, kindness and teamwork. He had had students go to the board and attempt to solve the problem. He had had the class applaud every attempt, and every attempt was a near-success. They had tried adding boxes, naming and numbering the lines, and making formulas. They had even tried to work the puzzle in their heads without paper. Failure was called failure, and they were beginning to see that the biggest failure was in not trying or in belittling those who did try but had not succeeded yet.

Children all but surrounded Robert and Beatrice in the cafeteria, a sea of children making their noises mingled together like sand and wind and contented waves on a beach with the tide still running in and the warmth of the sun filling the world for everything that had life. He looked away from

Beatrice, who sat across the table, and out over that sea and heard their murmur, and when she looked, too, he was glad. Their psalm—his and Paula's—came unexpectedly rolling over him like a great swell from far away, hurling itself on the shore in praise and then receding in thankfulness.

He wanted to recite it to her amid the noise, but did not, so he remembered instead: *Those who go down to the sea in ships, who do business on great waters, they see the works of the* LORD, *and His wonders in the deep.* He and Paula had seen, and that whole psalm—107—was theirs. He looked at Beatrice and then back at the children. "The puzzle was a great idea," he said. "I was able to do some pretty good things with it."

"I'm glad," she replied, smiling. "I was hoping you'd be able to use it."

For a few moments they both concentrated on eating, then she said, "How did you get into teaching?"

His immediate response was a glance and the arrangement of some black-eyed peas into something like a square on his plate. "My wife—was killed in a wreck—" Robert paused and retreated again into the silence that always came with those words, no matter how noisy the place where he said them might be. "We—" The cafeteria sounds returned; utensils were clacking into a bin by the handful. "We were house parents at a children's home for a number of years. The kids coming in kept getting more violent and disruptive, and our own children were being affected by them. The restrictions on what we could do kept getting tighter. We took turns going to a local college, we graduated, got our certifications, and became teachers in the public school system. When Paula was killed, I moved our son and daughter here."

"But why did you decide to teach in public schools?"

"Other than the family, it's the place of greatest need."

They resumed eating, then he asked, "What about you? Why did you choose teaching?"

"I haven't chosen it yet," she replied, looking around the room. "I'm considering it." Their eyes met. "I'm not sure it's worth the hassle."

He rested his fork. "Neither am I."

Her eyes darkened. "What will become—" Beatrice tilted her head to the side, "—of them?"

"They will be lost." With those words, he lowered his eyes to the table. "We—Paula and I—promised that we—" The sentence had become too heavy to complete.

Her words came matter-of-factly. "It's time to go, Robert." He looked up to see her smiling and smoothing the hair of a boy beside her as she gazed just over the boy's head. "Tell me, Allen—can the puzzle be solved?"

The boy jerked his eyes up into hers. "Yes, ma'am! An' *I'm* gonna do it!"

Beatrice looked at Robert and allowed her smile to fade. But something in her face did not leave. He thought of it as hope.

That afternoon, he was at the chalkboard explaining verbs. The intercom clicked on all over the school, and a woman's voice said, "This is Ms. Mayhew-Barr. I want to see Mr. Robert Farr in my office at three-thirty." There followed a lengthy pause. "Thank you."

The boy's hand was surprisingly small. As they shook hands at the door before going out to the bus, Robert Farr said, "Thank you, Robert, for your descriptive summary. It showed a lot of good thought." The boy grinned and bolted through the door, his rubber-soled shoes squeaking exclamation points down the hall. The teacher followed slowly, buttoning his overcoat against both the rain that was pouring outside and the gloom of the hall, as if within himself he could find the warmth and light to face the cold wetness of a world stripped of the sun. Bus duty. "Don't run," he muttered to other children detained for a few minutes after the three o'clock bell. *Don't run.* The thought was as effective as the words.

He should have already been out there, but Robert had forgotten. Honestly. *Honestly* was an important word, and he had really forgotten. The crumpled hat was out of the pocket of his overcoat and in his hand—well, his fist—and being alternately squeezed and then almost dropped. Pulling the thing down on his head with both hands—low over his eyes—he walked on, thinking again about working in a school full of women. He was the only man around except for three janitors.

Sure, he would admit it: he was worried; that's why he had forgotten. He was worried about being fired. *If Mayhew-Barr were a man*—This thing had been a long time building, and the school board would go along with whatever she wanted because the board was mostly men and Mayhew-Barr was definitely not ugly. The two women on the board would side with her on this issue because they, too, were "liberated and enlightened." He was through. History. But this time he would appeal. Just as long and as high as necessary. He *would* appeal.

He jammed both fists into the overcoat pockets until he heard stitches pop. The thought of fists smashing glass or jaws helped him to ease up. He would appeal, but the appeal would most likely have to go outside Wardensville, even though the town was "right on the buckle of the Bible belt." Robert knew that was a laugh; he had met only a few of the fifteen thousand residents, but none of them seemed to take to outsiders. Of course, most of those he had met were from the city's old families, like Mayhew-Barr. Mayhew Street was the main drag, and there was a Mayhew Park. Robert was through. But he would go down fighting . . . *If only she were a man*—His patience was paper thin, enough was— Robert shoved the door open and burst out into the rain, making a beeline for his assignment spot among the knot of children pushing onto one of the yellow buses lined around the circular drive. Exhaust fumes and the smell of rain vied with the chill for his full awareness, but fighting was the only way to go down.

A woman shouted from down the line of buses. "Farr! Robert Farr—stop that fight! Are you blind?"

He turned to see two of his boys flailing away at each other with flying fists, and nearly all the punches connected with resounding thumps. With a practiced movement, he grabbed them both by the collar and pulled them apart with a gruff, "Stop!" Looking at their welted faces and their beginning tears, he scolded, "Look at you! Both of you are going to have shiners tomorrow!" The rain was running down their faces as their glaring eyes began to soften. "You both know our rule—no fighting, especially between members of our class. We're family, remember? We'll deal with this tomorrow! Now, pick up your books and things from the mud and get on that bus!" They obeyed, and Robert turned around to see every child's face pressed against steamy windows.

"Justin won!" shouted one boy.

"He did not! Kevin did!"

Robert stepped up into the stairwell of the bus and nodded to the woman driver. "They both lost!" he said to the clamoring kids. "They lost control of *themselves*. Now get back in your seats." When they had more or less complied, he added, "Neither of their faces look like winners to me, and tomorrow, neither Justin nor Kevin is going to feel like a winner. Their faces are going to be bruised and sore. Their books are all muddy, and they're all wet. And they held up all the buses, so everyone will be a little later getting home." He gave each of the boys a final look of disapproval and got off the bus.

In a few minutes the last bus had disappeared around the bend toward town, and Robert stood watching rain-drops fall from the front of his hat in line with a tree about a hundred meters away. *Order . . . meaning . . . purpose: we always look for something to make sense, to have a purpose,* he was telling himself when he almost heard the command: *Order—arms!* As a man, the platoon obeyed . . . the crisp sound of weapons being grounded. Paris Island in the rain. The Mekong Delta in the rain. Wardensville in the rain. *Line up with the man in front. Line up your sights. Line up the bodies. Line up the raindrops. Fight . . . kill. Don't fight . . . don't kill. You had a good home, but you left! You're right! Left, right, left, right . . . line up. Order. Order—arms! Weapons: maybe they're only things that are ordered; maybe the rest just falls into place like boxes joined together with broken squiggly lines . . .*

Stop! he thought as he broke up the fight again in his mind. *Why break up fights? Why were we forced to fight Charlie with one hand and then to finally throw in the towel with the other? What was the purpose of so many deaths?*

Robert did an about face and started back to the door in an effort to stop the questions. Termination would be tough, and he wasn't going to have the luxury of being philosophical. A twelve-year-old boy and a ten-year-old girl weren't going to be fed, clothed, and housed by his spouting clichés and studying his navel.

Inside the building, he jerked the hat from his head and brought it down in a hard, chopping motion that sent a watery arch flying. He removed the coat as he went, crammed the hat into a pocket, and squished his way to his room, where he hung up the coat and sat down at the desk that he would soon be cleaning out. *What would Paula say if she were here?* Maybe he wouldn't be in this mess if she were still alive; she had been his stability in some pretty tough times. He looked at his watch: three twenty-five. Robert stood up, straightened his tie, and turned off the lights as he left the room.

His breathing rose and fell in time with his walking . . . why he shouldn't . . . left, right . . . why he shouldn't . . . so that upon reaching the office door, he was in control, felt in control as a matter of fact. *This is no time, there has never been a time, to have it out with Mayhew-Barr.* He would hear her and then leave, saying that he would appeal. He wouldn't tell Michael and Penny tonight. It shouldn't be effective immediately anyway, and he was *not* a fanatic; no one had ever called him that. Robert had obeyed the guidelines, except that he refused to say or teach that humans or any animals were products of chance. And the fact that he would not insert the word *other* before animals did nothing to win him friends in the educational field. Einstein had said it: God doesn't play dice with the universe. He walked by the office door and stood at the glass wall looking out at the rain. On purpose he had passed the office; *there must be a purpose—somewhere—even for Paula's death.*

Robert turned slowly from the darkening wall of glass and pulled his eyes from the rain. *There has to be.* So be it: to say that word and mean it must be one of the greatest acts of faith.

The sign read, *All visitors must report to the principal's office*, and that's exactly what Robert Farr felt like—a visitor. *Everything I know is somewhere else. I don't know nothing here.*

Hold on. Robert—hold on—for the children. He walked the few feet to the office door, opened it, went in, and hesitated a moment before closing it. The suite was empty; maybe everyone was in the copy room or a side office. The principal's office appeared to be empty, so he went to the door and looked in. It was.

This had happened before, somewhere a long time ago: a principal's office after school, but then it was not for his life, only a boys' fight, and she had called him a bully for starting it even though the other boy was bigger. Robert had been mad at his parents for mentioning divorce while they were arguing, he remembered later. After he graduated from high school, they had made good their threat.

And there is nothing new under the sun, he thought while choppers moved out overhead, . . . *and the sound of their wings was like the sound of chariots with many horses running into battle.* Sure, the writer of Revelation would have called them locusts. They ate up the lieutenant's words until only his mouth was left: *Charlie's out there . . . Charlie's out there . . . and he's dug in—*

He walked into the tent too young to cry or to be scared. *Corporal Farr reporting, Sir. We took losses, Sir. The platoon's gone. Semper Fi, Sir.*

They were guys he knew. Walloping backwards in pieces or dropping in place like they had suddenly remembered to die.

Again, Robert scanned Mayhew-Barr's degree: State University. Carol Sherril Mayhew. Master of Education, 1970. He turned to look out the window at the rain and the deserted circle where the buses had been. Where the choppers had been and where Charlie was . . . before, somewhere, a long time ago . . . *Semper Fi*—

"Mr. Farr," came his name from behind him—a woman's voice, familiar except for the tone of normalcy. Immediately, he faced her, and he noticed that she had a little smile that looked more than temporary. Her white teeth touched her lower lip for a moment, and her eyes had nothing of the hardness that he had always seen before.

"Yes, ma'am."

"Sit down," Mayhew-Barr said, though not with any sense of urgency.

"After you, ma'am."

She laughed. "Robert—" Her head tilted and her shoulder-length black hair shone like a raven's wing in the sun. "This is the twentieth century!"

"Okay." Robert sat down and watched Mayhew-Barr turn toward the side wall and slowly close her eyes.

"This has been a trying day," she offered quietly. An incredibly deep breath followed as she rolled her head upward and pushed her elbows far back. Then quickly, as if self-conscious, she dropped her arms and faced him. "Excuse me, please, I forgot," she said as she readjusted the bottom of her black sweater.

The seriousness of her face indicated that she might have been telling the truth. Here was an almost new thought: Mayhew-Barr was pretty . . . more than pretty, much more;

she was— "It *has* been trying," Robert replied over a pause that didn't fully yield to his thoughts.

Her smile gone, she sat down in a chair across from him and eyed his face for several moments. "Do you plan to go to the seminar on evolution?" she asked out of the blue.

"No."

"Why not?"

"It's about defending evolution, and I don't defend what I don't believe in."

Mayhew-Barr was smiling again. "Are you *afraid* to go?"

Tilting his head with a glance sideways, Robert decided to answer the intended provocation with the absurdity it deserved. "Yes, I'm afraid to go."

Her eyes widened.

"Now you know my secret. I'm afraid. I've always been afraid of seminars." His voice dropped slightly as he realized that he had nothing to lose. "It stems from something that happened a long time ago."

She surprised him by immediately asking, "And what was that?"

"You see, before I was born, my mother was frightened by a seminar. She never got over it. Since it was early in my fetal development, natural selection took over and kicked in dominant genes for seminarphobia. I mutated and eventually passed the trait on to my children. Since neither I nor my children have the ability to tolerate seminars, we will never be able to attend graduate school." He paused and glanced downward. "Because of that, we're doomed to extinction. I'm afraid this line of Farrs has gone as far as it can." Robert pretended not to hear her laughter as his eyes held hers with all the seriousness he could muster. "It's the law of the jungle, ma'am; only the fit survive."

He must have compounded her merriment, which had been increasing with every sentence, by continuing to look deadly serious as her shoulders shook and her eyes narrowed and filled with tears. Mayhew-Barr was out of control, her hands going to that beautiful face, her eyes closing, looking away and back at him; then she would lean forward even more as her laughter filled the room and his world at that moment. His senses drank in the sight and sound of her, the whiteness of her teeth, the raven hair spangling over dark eyes crying. He watched her take from his solemnity increased helpings of delight like a little girl who had discovered a hidden dish of candy.

For all of his unsmilingness, he, too, was laughing— somewhere—while his face stayed fixed by the choppers moving out again overhead and by the men he had known remembering to die somewhere in that jungle she could never know. Also, his face remained fastened, he knew, by instinct—as others called it—five years old.

Ms. Dunstal and the other secretary appeared at the door behind Mayhew-Barr with faces full of awful annoyance. Glowering at Robert, Dunstal demanded with her eyes an explanation of what was going on, and his nonchalant shrug blared those eyes into a most enjoyable fury. "We're gone!" she announced much too loudly.

The principal threw up a hand and managed through her laughter to say, "Fine." Dunstal stamped her foot and disappeared about two seconds before the slamming of the office door punctuated their departure.

Mayhew-Barr was beginning to recover, and Robert aided her by finally smiling; he didn't think he would be fired—today. She had wiped her eyes and was looking like the principal again, a recovered and reclaimed principal who had incited something in him he had thought was dead, and now he was feeling increasingly awkward.

"That was hilarious," she finally said.

"Thank . . . you," he responded, unwilling to resist the urge to play along the edge of the reason he was there.

Perhaps Mayhew-Barr didn't notice; she asked, "What do you find wrong with evolution?"

"It's simply not true."

"How do you know?"

"There are many reasons. Reputable scientists in many fields have written books explaining those reasons."

"Then they can't be reputable," she tossed back, then with an engaging seriousness asked, "Tell me—what is your main reason?"

"The main reason *I* reject evolution—actually, I have two main reasons, and neither of them is scientific."

"Of course. There can be no scientific reasons for rejecting the truth! But go on—what are your reasons?"

"First: the Bible reveals a great deal about the character of God. Survival of the fittest, as a means of creation—before humans sinned—is inconsistent with the character of God."

"Oh. Do you believe everything in the Bible?"

"I believe the Bible is the Word of God."

"That's amazing! No intelligent, educated person today believes that collection of primitive mythology!"

"I do, but it's not myth."

"Okay, go on," she said, obviously enjoying the exchange. "Second reason."

"To believe that life came about by chance is to believe that ultimately neither life nor anything else has any purpose whatsoever. That's a very arrogant piece of propaganda for a group of intelligent people to push on a gullible public. That's especially true in light of the fact that the *theory* of evolution is rendered totally impossible by the second *law* of thermodynamics!"

Mayhew-Barr blinked and momentarily frowned. "That's incredible!" she shot back. "You're qualified to teach science, and you actually believe the Bible *over* science!"

"Ms. Mayhew-Barr, true science and the Bible have no disagreements. There's no way evolution could be science, because science depends on *observation*. Evolution is philosophy—not science."

"You may call me Carol," came her quick reply. Then she said, "I find it amazing that you actually believe that collection of primitive writings!"

"The sun is primitive, but you believe it's there."

"I can *see* the sun. Let's talk primitive for a minute, Robert. You don't think we're close kin to other animals?"

"Not at all."

"Why? Are you afraid of the primitive instincts?"

He hesitated, looking into the depths of her eyes, telling himself that she didn't know him. "Yes," he replied as before, this time without any semblance of joking. "I'm afraid of what are called instincts. I've seen what they can do in the jungle . . . and other places."

"What can they do, Robert?"

Like a barren tree, dead and cold, emerging from the fog as one walks closer, the word came: "Kill."

"Yes. But that's not all."

"Carol," he replied, feeling the strangeness of her name on his tongue, "I don't believe humans have instincts."

"Really? Well, that's theoretical. What are you afraid of then, if it's not instincts?"

"What am I afraid of? Sin. I'm afraid of sin."

"Oh. I see." She looked down. "I'm not surprised. And *I* don't believe in sin."

"What do you mean, you're not surprised?"

"I mean . . ." She raised her eyes into his. ". . . that I thought all along you don't know how to have fun."

He inhaled deeply. "Go on."

"That's all." The fingers of her right hand went to the hem of her skirt over her crossed legs, and she watched them pick at it for a moment in little upward motions. She looked back at him as she smoothed her skirt. "I was right. You are afraid."

"Afraid of what?"

Mayhew-Barr smiled. "Oh, seminars, sin, and . . . other things."

Robert managed a smile. "I see," he replied, hoping his face didn't betray how much he did see and imagine and want . . . Wanting to say something to nullify everything that was happening, he could not; he sat, instead, struggling to meet her unblinking gaze.

"I think," Carol was saying, "you'll come around."

Robert had to look away, to break contact with her. The night was inverted by his scream. *Paula!* The last time he held her . . . *Hold on, Robert.* And he had, just as tightly as he could until he was pulled away.

"Carol—" Her name had been said. Carol. To tell her of the tree. About the tree he had held, cold and dead, instead of Paula. To press against the awful hurt that wouldn't go away, blinded in the headlights like an animal numbed by the cold, clinging to the hardness of the tree. Hold on, and he had tried, always to hold on, but there was nothing but a tree. Nothing but a cold, dead . . . barren . . . tree. Until now.

"Yes?"

"What?"

"You called my name, then just sat there like you were lost."

"Oh. I—well, I was thinking—"

"About what?"

"I don't know," he heard himself say. Robert felt shaky, so he tried a smile and a long glance away. "Maybe—" Honest words began to line up. "Maybe I was thinking about why I said 'Amen' over the intercom." His gaze returned to her. "I thought—perhaps I was thinking—that was the reason you asked me to come in."

"Of course."

"Was it?"

"Yes."

"I want you to know," he stated with a little hesitation, "that I appreciate your honesty."

She looked puzzled. "Why would I be any other way?"

"I don't know."

"What do you mean, you don't know?" she asked with an air of rapid detachment.

"I mean, you didn't waste time, you got right to the point of why you called me in."

Mayhew-Barr leaned forward and pointed a finger momentarily at the ceiling. "Now, listen, and get this straight! You're not going to sit in my office and call me a liar! If you—"

"No," Robert replied, shaking his head, "you don't understand. I'm not calling you a liar. You detest Christianity. *You* know that evolution in all forms is *absolutely* incompatible with the Bible and Christianity. You've said that when all is said and done, a theistic evolutionist is still an evolutionist. You go straight for the jugular, and you just did with me!" He paused at the widening of her eyes, but she had apparently lost her tongue. "You didn't beat around the bush. I find that refreshing, Carol."

"You!" the woman snarled at him through a mouth that was beautiful even in rage. "You find me refreshing, do you? You come in here to play—to play games—" Mayhew-Barr was again out of control and nearly shouting. "You're afraid! Afraid of everything. Yes, I hate your superstitious stupidity! I hate it!" She stopped to draw in several quick, deep breaths and in a steadier voice went on. "Yes, Robert! You're right! Evolution—in any form—would destroy your silly beliefs! But it's in now! And there's nothing you or your kind can do about that! You've lost, Robert Farr! Your faith is dead, your belief is dead, and you're dead! You're *dead*, Robert Farr—*dead*!"

"But my behavior isn't, and that bothers you."

"Yes! Your behavior is stupid, and you're stupid!"

"My behavior bothers you, Carol, because behavior *is* belief! So you know my belief isn't dead after all."

She was looking at him sidelong and working her jaw. "You're . . . crazy," she finally muttered.

"Who's afraid now, Carol?"

"Go to—"

"The seminar? That's where it originated, you know."

The woman stared at him for a few seconds, then a smile barely touched her face. He had ample time to guess her next words, and he was correct. "You are . . . terminated. You're history—dead history."

Robert's expectation of these words did not lessen the blow. Michael and Penny swirled to mind. He twisted his mouth and said, "Well, I'm not surprised. You see, that's the way many so-called scientists do business: get rid of what you can't explain. People like you, Ms. Mayhew-Barr, are the most frightened people in the world. You're afraid of the truth because you want to be your own god."

"Goddess."

"Yes. But you're the one who has lost. You see, Robert Farr is just another piece of evidence that you're afraid to face. You can't explain me so you call me crazy, stupid, and superstitious. You think I'm ill-informed, but I'm not. You *know* evolutionists are embarrassed by the lack of evidence, and you know that many eminent scientists know evolution is a hoax! Are you aware that Marquis de Lafayette had a perfect Neanderthal skull? Do you know that 'Lucy,' the skeleton said in the '70s to be a link between man and ape, was found almost two miles from that vitally important knee and that knee was dozens of meters lower down—"

"That's enough! We have nothing else to discuss."

"Didn't you call me in to talk about why I said 'Amen'?"

"That was my purpose, but we've reached an impasse, and I don't have time to hear excuses about why you violated the law by forcing a prescribed prayer on everyone in this school."

"May I have one sentence to explain? Just one?"

Pursing her lips, she nodded. "One sentence."

"The word means 'so be it,' and to me it means 'God's will be done'; it was force of habit."

"That's all?"

"That's all."

There was a long pause before she asked, "Would you go to the seminar to keep your job?"

"No."

"Then, I'm afraid—" She paused with a half-smile. "—that I'm going to have to . . ." There was another pause. "Place you on probation."

"I thought I had been terminated."

She inhaled deeply and put her head back, exposing her flawless throat. "*I* don't lose."

"I see."

Dropping her chin low, she replied, "You've made yourself a piece of evidence that you said I couldn't face. Well, I'm going to examine this evidence *very* closely! And I don't think you're going to—"

"Is that all?"

"That's all for now." She stood and extended her hand. Quickly Robert arose and took the hand, noting its softness and strength. "Thank you for coming by, Robert!" She resisted his attempt to shake hands. "And there *is* one other thing."

"What's that?"

She smiled warmly. "Happy birthday."

He glanced over her head and then into her sparkling eyes. "Thank you."

"That's more like it! See you . . . tomorrow."

And tomorrow, and tomorrow, and tomorrow, he thought with an anxiety that seemed to say it would have been better to have been fired. "So be it," Robert answered, releasing her hand. Hurriedly, he made his way out of the office, then out of the suite and down the silent hall toward his classroom to get his coat and reading glasses. As he walked, it seemed that every event in his life followed him like a pack of wild, dirty children clamoring and fighting and killing one another over something he couldn't give them because it was illegal.

For several steps, he closed his eyes to the familiar halls and tried to call back the fragrance of the rain while forgetting the exhaust of the buses. He couldn't do it. *There's no solution.* But he could—if he remembered another world far, far away in the spring when life was green and every day was as long as Christmas Eve. He put his hand out in the darkness and imagined that Paula was there to take it. And the halls went away, and there was no more echo. Loneliness was closed like a book that has been read and then is put away and remembered no more. Her hand had been in his, soft and strong. Only a minute ago, it seemed. Only a minute ago and not far away at all.

With so much evidence—he opened his eyes—*with so many Bibles, why does she have to have a life to test? Stuck back here out of the way with no solution—why?* If everything about her was wrong—and he knew it was—then why did he want her so much? Fragrance and fumes. In the doorway of his classroom, he stopped with closed eyes and the deepest longing for Paula that he could ever remember. Connelly wasn't here now. Nobody was here, so he cried.

3

Robert had chosen the stone house because, being small and in a not-really-desirable neighborhood, it was affordable and would not need much upkeep. It was also within comfortable walking distance of the private school Michael and Penny attended, and the elderly neighbors would keep watch over everything from their windows. These neighbors had become content, if not glad, to have the Farrs living in the old Shannon house and were usually happy to have Michael and Penny around to mow their grass, rake their yards, wash their cars, or run errands for them. At Robert's insistence, charges for mowing and raking and car washing were always set beforehand through serious negotiation and by the job. Other services brought in returns dependent upon the generosity of the persons served, Robert also insisted, and when the kids came home empty-handed, they were taught not to complain. "Remember when . . ." he would say, and there followed a recitation of undeserved benefits the three of them had received because of or in spite of Mr. or Mrs. So-and-So. The recitations would go on until the eyes of Michael and Penny had locked to form a bond of repentance and a plea for deliverance. He would laugh inside at the looks they gave each other, which he pretended not to see, and at times nearly break down from wanting Paula there. Now, mowing, raking, and washing cars—those negotiations were strictly the responsibility of the pint-sized entrepreneurs, as he called them. Of course, there would be and had been inconsistent rates among the clients depending upon which one looked or sounded scariest at the negotiation door. And these inconsistencies had been reported; more than once discontented clients had approached Robert, and each time he had absolutely and with terrible finality disowned his own children—as he overheard Michael and Penny say. Actually, all he had done was to send them back to face their accusers and make things right.

That night, the hardships he had inflicted upon them, both real and imagined, were all forgotten. At the candlelit kitchen table after dinner, Michael and Penny looked at each other, grinned, and then looked at him. That particular look didn't last long before they started singing, but it was another one of those things he felt he didn't deserve and would never forget. It was a miracle, as he thought of it, that he didn't get all mushy right there at the table.

"Happy birthday to you ... Happy birthday, dear Dad ... Happy birthday to you."

Under their instruction, he sat at the table while they left the kitchen as quickly as they could walk; Penny, like always, went first as ladies are supposed to. In those few moments, he felt something like an inner wind caressing all that had followed him down the halls of his memory this afternoon, and he thought of the wind of their going as it danced the flame of the single candle Penny had placed on the table when her face had looked so much like Paula's.

That wind had caused memories to stand up like children in his class when they played the game he called "The Old Times" so they would see—and maybe feel—how it was when the teacher entered the room in those days. Now they would do this and other courtesies only as a game. But not Michael and Penny. With his real family, responsibilities and manners were very important.

Concerning manners, Robert had learned that you don't show tears to people like Connelly, people who don't understand. But tonight . . . and if he did, or rather, when he did, it would ruin everything. Because he had led them and taught them to use their faith. And they were doing well because they were children. So Robert tried to pray and felt nothing, nothing but failure, a steady stream of failure. He could hear Michael and Penny returning, and the candle flame, steady and serene, blurred. He couldn't pray at his own table. Only that one awful word he had said over the intercom came to mind, and as he tried to wipe it away with the back of his hand, it wouldn't go.

They were blurs in front of his face with leftover Christmas wrapping paper swimming between them and himself, and Christmases were a nightmare—Somewhere a bell was ringing; somewhere children were saying, "Somebody's here! Somebody's at the door!" The flame leapt and danced before indistinct faces, and there could be no blinking.

No blinking as his voice said, "Don't move. I'll get it."

Robert got up and went quickly through the push-door into the dark and chilly hall, where he stopped to pull a handkerchief from his hip pocket and wipe his eyes. This done, he carefully refolded the handkerchief, replaced it, cleared his throat, and proceeded to turn on the porch light and open the door.

The familiar face had no name for a heartbeat; she was from somewhere else, and it seemed strange to see her. "Beatrice," he said finally. She stood in the light wearing a gray suit, all dressed up like maybe she was going to church. Though she wasn't smiling, she seemed about to, and she had something in her hands—a white box—and she was very attractive.

"Happy birthday. I made a cake and brought it by." The box was a little closer now.

"Well, ah—" She was the first woman, other than two neighbor ladies, to come here. "Bring it in!" His hand came up as though he was about to direct music, and he laughed. "Please—"

Her lips inclined toward a smile, and her eyes were so clear that he brought his hand up again like a boy with a yo-yo. No words came for him to say, but he didn't feel awkward either. Robert just looked at her there in the light and felt glad.

She was coming in, and he stepped back against the open door for her to pass, thinking about holding his breath because of the perfume he remembered, but he did not.

Instead, he closed his eyes that moment and lifted his head toward the light and breathed deeply knowing she would not see nor know that it was the sun he felt on his face by memory. She didn't look like Paula, and the fragrance was a little different, but— "Here, let me get the light," and his hand flew to the switch to bathe the little hallway in a decision he had not considered at all, from the day they had come until just then. It was bare, he knew, a hardwood floor with no rug, and chilly but clean. Beatrice stood with her back to him, waiting.

He closed the door, saying nothing but looking at her back and finding it altogether marvelous that she waited without saying anything. It was so wonderful that Robert had to stop and watch her. She didn't move, and something like joy so filled him that she blurred as the candle had and as Michael and Penny had. He reached in his pocket again and when his eyes were dry, he felt the silence ringing, and a time like Christmas, just a little, from long ago. "Here, let me get the door," he said, as he moved past her and pushed the door to hold it as widely open as he could.

Beatrice went past him to stand just inside the kitchen. Over her shoulder, he could see only the faces of his children as they gazed up in candlelit wonder, still holding their Christmas-wrapped presents and looking for all the world like a pint-sized angel and wise man. "Michael and Penny," he said, "this is Miss Bertram, an aide at Jefferson Elementary."

"How do you do, Miss Bertram," they said in unison.

"Fine. How are you, Michael and Penny?" Robert could hear the smile in her voice.

"Fine, ma'am."

"Fine."

"Well, I brought a cake, in case you don't have one."

Penny replied, "Oh, no, ma'am. We didn't have a way to get one, and we didn't have a mix."

Beatrice laughed. "Then it looks like I came at the right time."

"Perfect," Robert answered, "just perfect."

The children gave no sign of ever moving from their places, standing as they were with faces telling nothing in the half-light, holding on to their angel- and tree-wrapped presents, gazing up at this strange woman. "Please," Robert said, stepping around her into the little room, "come in."

Beatrice went to the counter, placed the white box there, and turned to him and the children, whose faces were still turned fully toward her though over their shoulders. Robert's eyes went to the fourth chair against the wall and under the table. He glanced at Michael and Penny, and now their eyes were fastened on his face. "Please go on," Beatrice said.

"Ah, yes," Robert replied with a good bit of relief. "I believe you have presents."

"Daddy—" Penny said.

"Yes?"

"Please sit down."

He nodded and the smile was not hard. "Of course." He sat where he was before, and Penny offered her present wrapped in blue crinkly paper printed with a multitude of angels. She wore a grin from ear to ear. "Why, thank you," he said, taking the gift and giving her a peck on the cheek.

Carefully, he undid the transparent tape and lifted a side of the wrapping to expose a thin, white paper covering which he lifted after he had looked around at everyone. The cellophane-enclosed white shirt, he lifted up for all to see. "Thank you, honey," he whispered, taking her in his arms and holding her with his eyes closed, feeling wetness on his neck and then on his cheeks. "Here, here," he managed, holding her at elbow's length. He produced the handkerchief and wiped both their eyes.

Composing herself, the little girl stepped back and said with a broken voice, "It's a nice white shirt."

He nodded. "Thank you, Penny." Clearing his throat, he looked at Michael, standing glassy-eyed and unblinking, gazing away at nothing he could think of. The boy came forward and held out a biscuit-sized package of Christmas trees on red. "Happy birthday, Dad," he stated bravely; then his tears released, and he was in his father's arms and so was his sister, and there was holding on and wetness and the darkness of closed eyes and crying, crying as they had that night, and holding on to each other.

He had not wanted this and had dreaded its happening, but Beatrice's presence fashioned the time into something that could only be called good. For her to see their tears was somehow right, and as with the psalm today at lunch, whatever had crashed down over the three of them was receding, and he felt its going as thankfulness in the warm sun of memory. Their faces were close but not touching when he raised a hand to each of their chins and smiled, and so did they. Then Robert knew that the nightmare was losing its power. The children seemed to know too and came close to a laugh, and then they did laugh. So he laughed, too, holding them again but not as tightly as before, and he called it, to himself, a miracle.

Robert looked at the woman and saw her face wet and glistening. Then she smiled, and he closed his eyes while slowly releasing the children. Just as deliberately, he opened his eyes to their faces. They were standing back now and looking at him as from so far away and yet, just then, so close. "Well," he finally said. Glancing down at the small package in Michael's hand, he asked as if he had just gotten there, "What have we here?"

The boy held it out. "Happy birthday, Dad."

Robert took the package and began the unwrapping, looking every few seconds from the present to Michael's face and back again, finding at every glance a smile grown larger. Dramatically, he lifted the last of the tree-lined redness to reveal a compass, its needle quivering directly at Michael, and Penny standing slightly behind.

"It's for when we go fishing and do stuff," the boy announced. "Also you can carry it around with you so you don't get lost."

"I'll always carry it, son," he replied, cupping a hand behind Michael's neck. He dropped the hand into a hand-shake with the boy, then reached around and took Penny by her hand so that brother and sister stood side by side. "You both have made me very happy. I love you both."

"I love you, too, Dad."

"I love you, Daddy."

"You knew exactly what I needed. I'll wear the shirt and carry the compass and always remember this night." Looking over at Beatrice, he added, "And now, I believe you said you brought a cake?"

"Yes." Without further comment, she began clearing the table, putting dishes in the sink.

Robert jumped up. "No, don't bother—we'll do that!"

Pausing with a plate over the sink, she said, "I'd really like to do this if you don't mind. In fact, we could all do it."

"Let her do it, Dad," Michael murmured with a sheepish grin.

"We'll all do it," Robert announced. The gifts and paper he put on the other end of the counter. "And young man, what happened to your manners?"

Michael squirmed. "I mean, it's your birthday and all."

Robert grinned. "Oh, I see."

In a few minutes the table had been cleared, the light turned on, and Beatrice had learned who the children's teachers were and what Michael and Penny liked to do on Saturdays. As for herself, she liked to ride one of her horses, and yes, she had two, Sugar and Spice, both girl horses, and Penny said that was because boys are so mean.

"Some are," Beatrice replied, "but not all."

The girl paused as though trying to remember something. "What's—" She looked up at the woman. "What's it like?"

"What's what like?" Beatrice asked.

"I mean—growing up—and being a woman?"

"It's nice, Penny, very nice."

"Well—" The girl glanced at her father and gave her brother an annoyed look. "Nothing." She went to the counter and balled up the wrapping paper. With a press of her foot, the trash can lid came up, she dropped the paper in, and the lid went down again. "I'm glad it's nice."

Beatrice continued gazing at the girl and nodded.

"But it's better being a man, isn't it, Dad?" Michael asked.

The girl spun to confront her brother. "It's two to two, now, Michael!"

"Whoa!" Robert injected. "It's *best* being who you are, the way God made you! Do you understand that, Michael?"

"Yes, sir."

"We—" Robert allowed a long pause as he stared at the window over the sink. His image stood in the darkness as it had in the light of the display case at school, and again, he tried to look beyond but could not. He thought, *In the image of God He created him; male and female He created them,* and said, "We are who we are for a purpose." Resting his eyes on Michael and Penny, he said, just as he had to his class from time to time, "There *is* a purpose. For everyone who will, there's a plan. We don't invent the plan, we find it. And we don't find it by denying *who* we are or by being satisfied with *what* we are. The fact that we need a compass means that there's a plan." Remembering Robert the student, he shrugged and added, "Well—that's all."

Beatrice opened the white box, pulling the cardboard lid back so that it rested almost level on the counter. There was a movement to see, and their guest herself stood gazing into the box with one of those looks on her face wanting someone to approve. Robert did, so much so that he stooped to examine the scene caught in plastic detail atop the oblong cake frosted as an American flag. On a little brown island in the center, a boy had just felled a barren tree. The tiny hatchet was clutched in his hand, and the boy's father stood beside him looking at the fallen tree with an arm around his son's shoulder. Robert straightened up.

"Do you like it?" Beatrice asked.

Without taking his eyes off the cake, he replied, "Very much."

Michael said, "It's George Washington, and he's just told the truth."

"It's beautiful," Penny added. "Did you make it, Miss Bertram?"

"Yes."

"It is . . ." Now Robert's gaze met the woman's. ". . . beautiful."

"Thank you."

There was the sound of a drawer opening, a clinking, and Michael was standing in front of her offering a knife, handle first.

"Somebody's still hungry," Beatrice intoned to the boy as her hand went out, hesitated, and then tousled his hair. Her eyelids dropped, she smiled in a way Robert had not seen before, and she put an arm around the boy's shoulder. The hand holding the knife dropped to his side, and he stood there beaming while Robert thought, *Penny, the score just changed.*

"Michael!" It was Penny's voice, "You're holding everything up! Now give her the knife so she can cut the cake."

"Why don't the three of us cut it?" Beatrice asked.

Robert got paper napkins, saucers, and forks, and in a

minute the three pairs of hands had produced the first slice, offered to her father with great ceremony by Penny, who apparently was too busy grinning to say very much.

Without ado, Robert placed his dish on the counter and pulled the table away from the wall. The kids noticed, but it wasn't like before. "Sit down," he said simply with their eyes hardly meeting as he held the back of the chair for her. She hesitated only a couple of seconds, but that hesitation was enough. It had been her chair and her table, but Paula had never been in this house anyhow. When they were seated, he asked them to join hands, and he gave thanks, pausing to reflect a moment or two before concluding, "Amen." With his first bite of cake, he shook his head in wonder and exclaimed, "You must have baked professionally!"

"No," she replied, "my mother taught me."

By the time Michael and Penny had each eaten two pieces of cake, and the crumbs were gone from all the saucers, and a two-liter bottle of soft drink had been found and emptied, Robert was talking homework. Mild and somewhat obligatory protests arose but then were abandoned under the outstretched arms of Miss Bertram, "the neatest," and her reassurance that if their father agreed, they could ride her horses, maybe this Saturday.

"We'll see," he said, and Michael and Penny hurried from the kitchen as if tarrying might change his mind. When he heard their doors close, Robert thought aloud to the woman across the table, "Your coming tonight was the best thing to happen to us in . . . well—in a long time."

"I'm glad."

The silence that followed spread out naturally around them as he gazed at her hands folded in front of her on the table. Gradually, it seemed, she was lifting that silence like a curtain with her presence and then with her voice while her hands waited. "What happened this afternoon . . . with Mayhew-Barr?"

"She fired me," he answered quietly, "then she put me on probation."

"I didn't think she would really fire you."

"Oh? Why not?"

"She's one of those people who's always had her way; she doesn't know any other way."

"So?"

"She can't stand even the thought of not getting what she wants. Firing you wouldn't destroy you. She wants to destroy you *and* your faith, because to her, Christianity is the sum total of all trouble-causing ignorance."

"How do you know?"

"I was born and reared in Wardensville, and I keep my eyes and ears open at work."

"You knew her before?"

"She's ten years older than I, and I know some of the people who've got in the way of Carol Mayhew *and* her father. He's Wallace Mayhew and was one of the original anti-God/anti-religion people in the state."

"Why?"

"His wife died."

Robert more than glanced at the darkened window. "Oh." There was no other sound, not even from the children's rooms. Michael would be at his little desk, and Penny . . .

"You didn't know these things, Robert?"

"No." Her hands were still on the table but not folded. "I—I'm an outsider. I knew the Mayhews were movers and shakers in town, but that's all."

"There are no Mayhews except Carol and her father."

"You said something that . . . well—"

"Yes?"

For some reason, Robert held his breath for a heartbeat before he responded, "You said Carol is ten years older than you—"

"That's right."

"Well, she's probably—"

"I'm thirty-four years old."

He felt his eyes widen.

"How old did you think I was?"

"Well, I . . . ah—" He laughed and for the first time felt awkward in her presence. "I . . . ah—twenty-two, maybe twenty-three."

Her laughter was genuine music, and her shoulders shook while her eyes called something to him that moved his hand toward hers; but she had not seen, so slowly he drew it back. Too soon, the laughter was over, but her smile remained as if it would never go, then her eyelids almost closed for that instant when he knew she was beautiful. And now she was looking at him and telling him with her eyes that she knew about that instant. "Thank you," she said softly.

Robert nodded and looked down for what seemed a long and troubled time, and when his head raised, she was looking at him. "After high school, I helped run my parents' farm for three years," Beatrice said. "We grew soy beans, corn, and raised steers, and I saved money and went to State the next four years, helping on the farm during the summers. I had an older brother, Daniel, who was killed in Vietnam. So I sort of tried to take his place to help Mom and Dad. They still have the farm, but we don't do much with it anymore. Now I have an apartment."

"You don't owe me an explanation."

"I don't mind. And besides, I want you to know. After college . . ." A smile came over her face. "I tried my hand at being a saleslady in a department store." A little laugh followed. "Two years and I don't know how I lasted that long! Then I became engaged and went back for my master's degree. My engagement lasted until I graduated, then his mother broke it up. She was very possessive. I took a year off for travel, and when I came back to the States, I worked in a day-care center in Florida for nearly four years. Private schools looked to be the place where a teacher could make a difference, so I came back home to give it a look."

"Why did you come to Jefferson? As an aide?"

"Jackson Level and Shadley had no openings."

Robert sat there feeling flashes of impressions here and there in his brain like rocket and mortar fire incoming at night, illuminating for bare instants those parts of reality occupied by a jungle tree or barbed wire and sandbags. His eyes would hold them afterward until fragments of world were bursting all over the compound, strobe lighting in gray smoke and black, men running—frozen in that instant— running—frozen—shooting—*Charlie's coming in*. Strobing black flashes on blinding white blackness—running—frozen—firing, firing—rock bands with concussion booming out of blacker splotches dotted with flashes of blindness, throbbing the earth in the total spectrum of chaos, shooting, explosions, screaming, and—"What outfit was your brother in?"

"One hundred and first airborne. You—were in Vietnam also?"

"Yes. How did you know?"

"The same way I knew this is your birthday. I looked at your application in the files."

"Why?"

"From time to time I'm in the office, and occasionally I hear what's being said. Some other things are not hard to figure out. I've been praying for you for some time, Robert." Beatrice paused and ran a finger over the handle of her fork. "You don't know it," she continued, looking now into his face, "but you've helped me more than you could guess. Because of you, I've started studying my Bible again, and my faith has been strengthened."

"Well—I'm glad for that."

"You say that as though there are some things you're not glad about."

He could tell from her face and tone that she understood. "Yeah."

"Stacy Robertson, who works in the office, is a Christian. As far as I can tell, there are two other teachers in the whole school who actually believe the Bible. There are many who laugh and say they're Christian, but there's no evidence in their lives."

Robert leaned toward her on his elbows. "What makes Mayhew-Barr tick?"

"Status. What she perceives as power. Everything she is, she learned at home, and of course, the public school system and the university completely reinforced all of that. Her mother's death didn't make her father an atheist. He was that way before; he just used the situation to justify his life-style."

"Which is?"

"Do anything you want to do, no holds barred, and don't look back."

"Is Carol an atheist?"

"I don't think so. She would, I think, call herself an agnostic. But I believe she has you in her sights, Robert! And I also believe . . ." Beatrice glanced down as she ran a finger over the tine of the fork, then locked her eyes into his, ". . . that she can be *very* persuasive."

Robert hesitated, then quietly replied, "I know."

Now Beatrice paused. "She's dangerous, Robert." Her hand moved a little closer to his on the table. "She's going for everything, and she has no rules."

Robert looked away, wanting to close his eyes to everything except the woman across the table. Her face was before him as he looked again at the window and the doorway's reflection, and the crossing lines of panes superimposed with so many would-be amoebas in his memory and his name as she had said it in the light against a background of darkness. But he was in the light because *God is light and in Him is no darkness at all.* And Beatrice was in the light, and Robert wanted her . . . *and the blood of Jesus Christ His Son cleanses us from all sin.*

I'm afraid of sin, he had said.

I don't believe in sin . . . I thought all along you don't know how to have fun . . . I don't lose.

Carol. He had said her name to her, and . . .

"Robert—"

He came back to her, to her face and her eyes, and it was there he needed to be as she said softly a word from so far away in time and place—But not with her mouth. *Somebody's still hungry,* she had said. And over and over the brownness of her eyes kept whispering that one feeling: home.

The softness of her lips moved. "I've prayed for you. I still do."

"Please, tell me that again."

"I've prayed for you. I still do."

His eyes closed. Her soft words were stronger than the stone house. A man could live in them. A man could . . .

"Robert, I'm going."

Looking at her, he shook his head. "Please, don't."

"Yes. I have to go." With that, she got up and took the dishes and utensils to the sink. "I would wash these, but it's getting late. I think you understand."

He stood. "Yes." Then he smiled. "I understand."

"Tell Michael and Penny that I said good night."

"I shall."

A comfortable silence descended as they stood there, then she started toward the door. When she was very close to him, he said her name and she stopped. Her eyes were straight ahead. "Thank you," he said softly, then pushed the door open to the hall. Robert followed her through the hall and walked her out to her car where they said good night and shook hands. He watched her drive away and then looked up at the sky. The clouds were gone, and even with the street light, he could see the stars. He wiped an eye, but the tears were not like before.

4

For perhaps the hundredth time, the entire day of his forty-fourth birthday had wound itself throughout the rooms of his mind as a long, continuous line whose end joined so imperceptibly with the beginning that he ceased to see the connecting as extraordinary. It was a whole; it made sense, and it was his. His life, he had thought in the beginning after a boy in his class had talked about a certain fishing trip.

And so it seemed to be, making sense only at the close of the day when she said she had prayed for him. The sense that it made, however, Robert did not try to put into words because—perhaps—they were not his words to know. It was a matter of faith—the substance of things hoped for, the evidence of things not seen—so what words could he use to tell what he knew about that which cannot be known on earth?

This time Robert did not wonder how he could have doubted, nor did he feel shame any more than a battered and dazed fighter feels shame for his wounds when he has beaten a vicious opponent. Yet, by no means did he think or feel that anything was over, or that victory was in sight. It was just certain, that was all—this victory—and it would not even be his when it came. That surely would not make sense to *his* opponents. But he knew now, more than before, that it would come. So he told himself, this Thursday morning, pushing knuckles into the pockets of his trousers, that a new day had dawned. There were no children, not a bus, not anyone to be seen anywhere out the classroom window, and the sun was about to shine. He hunched his shoulders as close to his ears as he could. No matter what might happen to him—his next breath was a deep one—no matter what might happen—

It was a matter of faith. Her own faith had gotten stronger. . . . *The evidence of things not seen.* Evolution has no evidence, no "missing links." Hadn't he plodded through *Origin of Species* and accepted every word as inspired by the scientific method? In college. And Bertrand Russell's *Why I Am Not a Christian.* And Nietzsche, Machiavelli, Rousseau, and Descartes. Then came his father's heart attack. And later, his mother's cancer, and afterward the emptiness when they were gone. But all along Paula's faith and patience had been there waiting.

Then . . . Vietnam.

Paula had lived her faith every day, and finally Robert had listened to her when she told him how he could, too. Like a child, he had begun to know life, love, and trust for the first time as an adult. Then, in his arms, she had left him the only way their promise allowed.

Robert dropped his shoulders into a natural stance, his

hands still in his pockets. Turning the compass over a couple of times between the fingers of his right hand, he thought of Michael and Penny and how they never really left his mind. His hand closed over the instrument. Yes, he too had been an agnostic going around saying, "We can't know," until one day he did know—not the purpose that his former faith had denied but the fact that there *is* a purpose. Paula had been the instrument, the compass, the one human who had been used to point him to the God he would come to know as she knew Him: as the Father.

That barren tree out there would live again. In fact, it was not dead even now. But another tree, close to the building, was dead. Decay had started; it should be cut down.

"Robert." If a sound could be both unexpected and expected at the same time, that word was. It was Mayhew-Barr. She was behind him; he guessed that she would be wearing a red coat that reminded him of a fox hunter's except that it was shorter. And it would be open with the ruffles of her white blouse overlapping its edges. Her skirt would be black as would her stylish boots, which didn't make any noise when she walked down the hall. He turned and saw that he was right on all counts. Her mouth was slightly open, unlike earlier when he thought she had not seen him coming into the school.

"Yes?" Now he waited for her to say why she had told him yesterday she wanted to see him.

"We have a problem." She walked slowly toward him as he watched her face. "There's been a complaint—well, there's been two complaints," she murmured before crossing her arms as if she were cold, rubbing her upper arms, and then leaning against his desk.

"What about?" he asked in order to fill the space, thinking again as he had yesterday when she had said, *We need to get together in the morning,* that the worst could be a long time coming.

"Your prayer."

He put a foot up on the seat of a front desk and leaned on an elbow across his knee. "Okay."

"Do you deny that you prayed?"

"No."

Her eyes widened, and he saw her knuckles whiten on the edge of his desk. "Robert!"

When it seemed that she would spin toward the door, but did not, he answered again, "Yes?"

"What's wrong with you? You did *not* pray! You just said one word! Why can't you say that's all you did, that that was all you intended? This thing could be—so simple!"

"Carol—I prayed. I prayed over the loudspeaker. I prayed for all the world to hear. I prayed one of the most profound prayers of my life. I'm guilty."

She looked at him and shook her head so that her hair swung back and forth under her chin. "You're crazy . . . that's what you are! We could say that you just forgot yourself—"

"I did."

"—that you made a slip of the tongue—"

"Carol?"

"What?"

"Why did you say 'we'?"

She blew an exasperated breath through tight lips. "You don't understand anything, do you? This is *my* school! I'm in a constant battle refereeing teachers and parents, teachers and teachers, and parents and parents! We have first graders who bring knives and guns to school; we have big-time drug abuse! Natasha James was the fourth student death this year. Connelly talked one boy into giving her a bomb he had made—a *bomb!* Most of our kids are sexually active!" Her voice fell but became even more distinct. "Phillips found a sixth grade boy and girl behind the gym mats!" Mayhew-Barr surveyed him from under heightened eyebrows. "That's why I said 'we'! *I'm* in charge of this school! What happens on this property is my concern, and now you've caused this prayer trouble and it involves me!" After pausing for a breath, she added, with a glance at the floor, "It was *my* phone that rang."

Robert turned two words over in his mind, *on cue,* but he did not say them. Instead, he stood facing her, his weight on both feet. He pushed his hands back into his pockets and tilted his head. He turned the compass over in his mind. "All the trouble—" he said, looking over her head at where the cardboard George had been and then full in her face, "do you think it was caused by people in these kids' lives *praying?*"

Her answer was a continuing cold stare.

"Or could it be that the trouble comes from an organized hostility *and* conspiracy against Christianity and its values on the part of our government, the educational system, and the media?"

The woman pushed away from the desk, her clenched teeth hardening her face into a knot of anger. She took a step toward him and literally spat out the word, "Conspiracy!" then followed with, "You're paranoid! Tell me, Mr. Dark Ages—" Her hand swung around to point to his desk behind her. "—have we bugged your desk? Are we beaming brainwashing rays at all the schools and homes? You *are* crazy! You need psychiatric help!" She went silent under a heavy breath.

"I don't know about the desk," Robert answered calmly, "but yes, brainwashing waves are being beamed at all the schools and homes."

Her mouth fell open.

"It's called television."

Staring, she shook her head. "Cultural retardation and mental illness are so insidious!"

"Let's be pragmatic. Twenty years ago—"

"This is *not* twenty years ago! I don't want to hear about the dark ages!"

"Being a principal and a teacher was much easier then."

"Progress doesn't come from making things easier."

Robert almost stifled a flash of anger. "Do you call children killing each other 'making progress'? What about making bombs, and having sex in the locker room? Are those things progress? Do you call it progress when a majority of our students leave high school without being able to understand the directions on a can of soup? Is it progress when one fourth of—"

"I'm not going to listen to any more of this."

"Do you call AIDS progress, Carol?"

Her lower lip curled up between her teeth for a second before she quietly inquired, "Why do you ask that?"

"It isn't hard to figure, from a few attitudes, actions, and comments—AIDS is in this school."

"Don't—" Mayhew-Barr glanced at the door and nearly whispered, "Don't say anything! I mean, nothing! There's no need to spread panic!"

"What about people's rights to know that their health and lives are in danger?"

The woman raised both fists in a gesture that deteriorated into helplessness. "*Please!*" she hissed. "Don't say anything!"

"Carol, why is AIDS a federally protected disease?"

"Robert—*don't* say anything!"

"Do you think we've been told the truth about casual contact?"

Her fists became quivering hands that he thought she was going to press against her ears, but in a heartbeat, she was inches away and they were imploring in front of his face. "Don't hurt me, Robert," she whispered, and he felt her breath on his cheek and smelled it and thought of spring and a soft hush of night. Her eyes descended and perhaps closed. Pouting, her lip hid her snow-white teeth before curling again between them.

He fought the almost overpowering urge to gently lay his hand along her face and then hold her too tightly for her to breathe, and then he would allow her to breathe . . . "What about your husband?" Robert said quickly.

Her eyes flew open into his. "What about him?"

He let his face answer.

"He's not a prude, if that's what you mean."

"I mean, you *do* have a husband!"

"So—what's that got to do with AIDS? In fact, what does that have to do with anything?"

Robert took a reluctant step backward and felt his heart pounding like a man running. Again, he put a foot up on the seat of a student's desk and thought something about a defensive posture.

"Robert, are you going to say anything?"

He shook his head. "No."

Mayhew-Barr's eyes closed momentarily, and she took another deep breath and slowly let it out. "Thanks."

"Do you believe me?"

"Yes."

"Why?"

"That's just the way you are."

"What? Can you believe the word of a crazy man? A man who's culturally retarded . . . mentally ill?"

"I believe you."

"I want to know why."

"Forget it."

"I'm not going to forget it. I want to know."

"Why should you care about my motives? Why should you care about me? *Do* you care about me, Robert?"

"As a person, I care about you. Why do you trust me?"

"I don't." She turned toward the door and stood there—like she was in the sun and it was shining in a wooded glen filled with green trees and yellow jonquils. She had just heard a bird and was feeling the wonder he felt, a wonder they shared. She turned to him. "I don't," she repeated with a sad face. "Anyhow, I was right. Here was better than the office. And I've got to get back. There's something else, but we got sidetracked." She looked away, seemingly at nothing, and said emptily, "There's an informal meeting tomorrow afternoon of two or three school board members. I want to resolve this without a mess. It's at five-thirty in my husband's law office. Can you be there?" She brought her eyes back to his.

"I suppose that I'll have to."

"Yes, you'll have to be there. This is very serious, Robert." Some fleeting change touched her face, then she was gone without a sound.

Traffic was seldom heavy in Wardensville, but Friday afternoons— Well, you couldn't say unless you were out there and part of it. The big jam always came at four-thirty where Washington and Mayhew Streets merged, but that was nothing compared to Peachtree in Atlanta at the same time. Robert's father used to say that a lot of people were still trying to get away from Sherman. Most of the man's attempts at humor came to nothing, but Robert knew now that it wasn't his father's fault. What wasn't his fault—his corniness? Or the divorce?

The man had been right. People were still trying to get away from some kind of Sherman. That's what he said, but then it hadn't meant a thing. When he baited the hook, Robert the boy watched his hands. They were big and a little scary because they seemed like such strange hands. But when Robert looked up, he saw the man's face, and it started out being scary, too. But wrinkles appeared around his eyes, and it got all right. Because the man's eyes moved ever so slowly to Robert's face like he was getting ready to share a big secret. Then the man smiled.

The sun getting ready to come up at the end of Peachtree was like nothing the boy had ever seen . . . quiet, nearly deserted despite so much industry and hustling bustle towering over everything. Buildings, tall, like standing around on tiptoe trying to catch a glimpse of the sun. And some of them had—all gold around the tops like big, old crowns. But when his father smiled, the sun had been on his face.

The red-mouth hula popper had finally worked just like the man said it would. The bass was huge—as long as from his fingertips to his elbow—and shaking its head in angry disagreement. Just big enough, the man said, and Robert wondered later if his dad could have meant something besides the fish from the way he had looked at him. Later, the boy knew. He had become a man without knowing it. That was the secret, and the day Robert knew, that night he cried. But his mother had fixed their breakfast. Why couldn't it have worked?

Always, his parents had never really gotten along. So much so that the boy hadn't seen how it could work. Becoming a man didn't add anything in the way of new knowledge, just new questions, so that one day his mother asked about what had started the fight that caused the principal to call him a bully. Only his mother wasn't supposed to know about the fight. And Robert had said he didn't see how it could work either, because—then—he just didn't know any other way. The morning the choppers moved out he remembered that breakfast she had fixed and the sun on his dad's face.

Barr, Watkins, and Craynor Law Offices, said the sign, said everything, even all the other buildings on Mayhew Street huddling together in lengthening shadows—or they could have said that for all Robert knew. Only one sign, a couple or three square feet, on the side of the building. *Two or three school board members. This is very serious, Robert.* He parked his seven-year-old Toyota facing the building between a new Mercedes and a new Cadillac. Five-twenty. Ten minutes. He shut the engine off, put the key in his pocket, and sat there. In the rearview mirror a guy was walking toward the door of the law office, his red tie and pepper-gray hair blowing nonchalantly. His suit was blue, he carried nothing in his hands, and he walked like a man about to enter a circus. Robert realized that he was doing what psychologists call projection and focused his attention on the brick wall in front of him. Now, he was facing reality, he told himself.

When the man was gone, Robert took a manila envelope from the seat beside him, opened the door, and inhaled the amber air of sun flung across old brick stores with windows foreshadowed into shards of turned-away reflections. The street lay dark like a dead limb, damp and half-buried among golden leaves towered over by white-barked trees, smooth and clean in their coldness. The little wind felt good to breathe and charged with life. It touched him, soothing, reassuring, and Beatrice was praying for him even now. Last of all it tousled his hair, and he smiled to himself. Her face came again to mind, or at least more clearly emerged, for now she was never out of his thoughts either. But it was the same look she had given him when Allen had said he was going to solve the puzzle and the same look he had last seen on her face twenty minutes ago. He walked leisurely; it was good to breathe the cold air.

The building was brick and had no windows except for a plate glass one in front looking out on Mayhew Street. That window was tinted so you couldn't see in, and so was the door on the right. Lettered on that door were the names of the firm's members: Z. Cyrus Barr, Winston M. Watkins, and Alexander A. Craynor. Robert had never been in before, but he didn't pause before pushing the door open because those inside could probably see out. The door made no sound closing behind him, squelching street noises to oblivion and sealing the fluorescent-brightened reception area into a concentrated smell of leather, paper, and perhaps ink. There was a counter for him to stand at while he waited for a woman's gaze to break free of several sheets of paper stapled together at the top left corner. She was standing, apparently arrested in mid-stride by the document, behind a desk covered with stacks of similar looking papers. Almost, she would lift her eyes only to succumb again to a turned page.

Since no one else was in sight and he hadn't made any noise coming in—but she should have heard the cars going by outside when the door opened—Robert took the opportunity to look around. There was another desk with a brown chair on wheels several feet away, an array of black file cabinets, and a waiting area near the end of the counter with two black leather chairs and a couch. A brass lamp, shaped like a Grecian urn, stood on a low table that appeared to be mahogany with a pool of light enclosing magazines fanned out under a cream-colored shade. The carpet was green, the walls looked like the table turned into paneling, and there were pictures in wide black frames: a chalet scene, and a mountain with snow on top hazed pink by the setting sun. "Excuse me—" Robert offered.

"Yes." Still the woman did not look up.

"I have an appointment with several school board members here at five-thirty."

"Your name?"

He made no answer, watching her as she continued to read. In a few moments she looked at him, and he said, "My name is Robert Farr."

"Have a seat."

He sat down and the woman disappeared down the dusky hall to the far left. Seconds later she was back at the counter saying, "Go on back. They're all there—waiting for you."

Robert stood up, courteously thanked the woman, and started toward the back of the building. The doors of three offices along the right side of the hallway each had a plaque bearing the name of an attorney. The only office with an open door was that of Cyrus Barr, and the man sitting at the desk Robert remembered seeing somewhere, probably a restaurant. They nodded to each other, and Robert kept walking.

The hall opened into a mahogany conference room where he paused in the doorway. He was surprised to see Connelly here. Three of the five faces around the long table appeared to have been stamped from the same irksome die. Except the man at the far end and Mayhew-Barr; she could have been playing poker given her lack of expression. The man at the far end was the only person he did not recognize, and he was the man Robert had seen walking toward the building. He was getting up and beginning to smile.

"Mr. Robert Farr, I assume," announced the man from the rearview mirror.

"Yes."

"Have a seat—please." Robert complied at his end of the table, and the man, still smiling, looked briefly at everyone there, cleared his throat, and walked behind Robert, closed the door, and returned to stand at the other end of the table.

"Now—" He sat down and folded his hands into a steeple in front of him. "My name is Allen Johnson. I've been asked to fill the unexpired term of Rocky Fearing, who died a while back. I was also asked to moderate this meeting by Superintendent Spivey." Johnson pushed his hands forward and watched his interlocked fingers stand up. Then he disjoined his hands and removed them from the table. "I believe everyone here knows everyone else." His smile disappeared to return with his next word: "But—let's go around the table and give our names."

"Carol Mayhew-Barr," she said from Johnson's right with a transitory smile.

"Woody Franklin," stated a man Robert had met briefly, a man whose brown hair was parted high on the right to terminate paintbrushlike against each ear. Franklin seemed to be watching everything and ever ready to do something with his right arm.

"Connelly," stated the woman on Johnson's left. "Just—Connelly."

The last man said, "Fred Stuart," and raised a couple of fingers.

Four vacant chairs sat on either side of the table between

Robert and the others. "Mr. Farr," Johnson began, "I want to make it clear that our purpose in being here today is threefold: information, communication, and understanding. I sincerely hope and fully believe that this meeting will resolve a misunderstanding and that we will go forward as a unified team without the necessity of any action by the board."

Robert replied, "I hope so," and Connelly leaned back to give a little negative shake of her head as she stared down at the table.

The moderator continued, "There have been two significant complaints about a prayer you allegedly prayed over the loudspeaker at Jefferson Elementary School where you are a fifth grade teacher."

Connelly spoke up, "Mr. Johnson?"

"Yes?"

"I want to say that in addition to those complaints—by very influential parents, I might add—there are others! I myself have one! I was highly, highly offended! And there are other teachers and workers in Jefferson Elementary who were also highly, highly offended. Some of them were downright incensed that this man—" Connelly leaned forward fixing Robert with a pointing finger "—should do such a thing!" The woman flopped disgustedly back in her chair and muttered, "And, he's supposed to be a teacher!"

Johnson rejoined to Robert, "Ms. Connelly is here, by permission, because she indicated that she had certain other complaints to introduce."

"I see."

The moderator pressed his lips together then said, "Mr.

Farr, I believe your alleged prayer was composed of one word, 'Amen.' Is that correct?"

"Yes, sir."

"Well, I took the time to check out some of the things that have been said, and the word is indeed from the Judeo-Christian setting. In fact, the word is the same in Hebrew, Greek, and Latin, the languages used to write the accusation against Jesus Christ that was attached to his cross . . ."

"See!" injected Connelly. "What did I say? The man is a fanatic who's illegally pushing an archaic—"

"Just a moment," Johnson said with ringing firmness in his voice. He turned to meet her eyes. "I, too, am a Christian!"

Connelly's breath miscarried, and she sank back in the chair to scan the ceiling with rolling eyes. Woody Franklin's arm was more restless. Carol's eyes found Robert's like a long-ago high school quarterback who had found him in the end zone from five yards out, and she gave only a hint of a nod.

Connelly's left hand fell away from the arm of her chair, and she leaned over and came up with her purse which she tossed on the table and from which she withdrew a pack of cigarettes.

"Connelly," said Robert, "please don't smoke. You know the reports about the effects of passive smoking."

The woman glared down the table at him with her closed mouth working into varieties of lines and puckers. One of those lines froze, and she nodded with icy deliberateness and slowly replaced the cigarettes and returned the purse to the floor while staring at him all the while through the whites of her eyes.

Stuart let out a long, audible breath, and it seemed none of the others were breathing.

"Remember—" Johnson's word hovered over the table until somebody's hands moved and there was a shifting of feet. "Christianity is not on trial. A person's faith, or lack of it, is a matter of that individual's decision. We are here to determine if Mr. Farr has, at any point, gone beyond what has been established as appropriate behavior for a public school teacher."

"What about," said Connelly, lifting her chin and gradually bringing her eyes around the table to end with a sidelong look at Johnson, "fondling children? Both boys and girls?"

The volume of silence that followed built on the tempo of an increasing heart somewhere in his ears. Carol's head bowed and her fingers hastened across her forehead to her thumb. Her hair swung back and forth under her chin. "No." She raised her head and leaned forward beside the moderator to confront the other woman. "You're *dead* wrong this time, Connelly!"

"Am I?" The woman nodded knowingly, "Am I, Carol?"

The principal leaned in front of Johnson. "Just what are you getting at?"

A little smile prefaced her answer. "I *know* what I've seen—and I *know* what I've heard!"

"Just *what* have you seen and *what* have you heard?"

Mayhew-Barr demanded, thrusting her head sideways in front of Johnson's face.

Connelly leaned back and fastened her eyes on Robert. "That would probably be a matter to take up before the entire school board—but I *will* say this: I have seen Mr. Farr put his hands on children of both sexes in an inappropriate manner and have heard him say personal, inappropriate things to them."

"I have never done either of those things," declared Robert. "Never."

"Do you deny," responded his accuser, "that you have embraced probably every child in your class, smoothed little girls' hair, put your face against theirs, and told them they are pretty? Do you deny that you have embraced little boys and told them how strong they were—even manly? Do you deny doing those things, Mr. Farr?"

"No. I do those things because—"

"Whatever you *say* your reasons are makes no difference! I—and others in that school—maintain that you *enjoy* those contacts! I don't want to be more explicit than that at this time. Also, I—and others in that school—maintain that what *we have seen* is only the tip of the iceberg!"

"You're crazy!" Mayhew-Barr shot back. "This is absurd!"

Connelly glanced toward her but probably saw only the side of Johnson's head. She quickly looked straight ahead, and the fear in her eyes was unmistakable. "I don't want trouble with you, Carol."

"Well, you've *got* trouble with me!" Sitting upright in her chair, she added, "Big time!"

"Carol," the other woman said, apparently looking at the wall behind Robert, "I should point out that a majority of the staff and teachers back me on this point."

Surprisingly, the principal laughed, a deep, shoulder-shaking, white-teethed, beautiful laugh. "Okay." She added a chuckle and repeated, "Okay."

Now Connelly's forehead was all disjointed lines, and her blanched face lurched as she swallowed and appeared to be readying for a topple to the table. But she recovered to sit there removing lines one at a time by gradually lowering her head and almost closing her eyes.

Franklin broke the silence. "We'll certainly need to very thoroughly look into these allegations!" He fixed Robert with a stare and then went on to other faces. "This is serious! Very serious! Very serious, indeed!"

"It *is* very serious," chimed in Stuart.

"It's nonsense!" Robert replied. "This whole thing is utter nonsense!" Every face in the room was aimed at him except two: Mayhew-Barr seemed to be studying the table midway between them, and Johnson tilted his head kindly forward for him to proceed.

"I have never done anything with any child that many other teachers who care about—" Again, Mayhew-Barr's eyes found his. "—those for whom they are responsible—their children—haven't done. The record will show that I have reported numerous cases of child abuse. A number of convictions have resulted from my reports, including several involving incest.

"Every year children come into my class who are afraid of men. Some of these children have been beaten severely. I don't know any other way to handle so many impossible situations than to let them know that I care, and I care enough to run the risk. I've never touched a child or said anything of a personal nature without a continuing prayer in my heart and mind: Lord, may I do the right thing; may I say the right word; may *Your* will be done—"

There was a moment's pause, then Connelly spoke up. "That brings us back to the straw that broke the camel's back: your prayer! However you may try to appeal to childhood innocence and vulnerability, you are a dangerous man! How much clearer can it be? You admit that you pray continually to your God that you will do His will—with public school children! This is in violation of separation of church and state! What more evidence do we need! What ... more ... evidence ... do ... we ... *need*?!"

Mayhew-Barr's gaze had fallen back to the middle of the table. "May I respond?" asked Robert.

Johnson answered, "Go ahead."

"I'm going directly to the heart of the problem that brought us here today and try to focus only upon the crux of our disagreement.

"Let me begin by quoting the First Amendment to the Constitution of The United States:

Congress shall make no law respecting an establishment of religion, or prohibiting the free exercise thereof; or abridging the freedom of speech or of the press; or the right of the people peaceably to assemble and to petition the Government for a redress of grievances.

"Concerning that amendment, we all agree on one thing: it is against the highest law of the land for our government to sponsor or favor one religion over another. I will show how this law has been scandalously and shamefully violated by our government and how this violation has led to the near moral collapse and academic failure of our public school system."

Franklin slapped the table loudly. "Ridiculous! Ridiculous! Ridiculous!" he exclaimed with wild eyes flashing. "We don't need to sit here and listen to this stupid fanatic tear down the government of the United States and tell us how to run our schools! I say let's sever him here and now and be done with him *and* his malarkey!"

"Woody," Johnson responded, "the man is entitled to be heard. It's only fair to—"

"Don't you tell *me* what's fair!" Franklin exploded. "You self-confessed rednecked bigot!" He leapt to his feet, sending his chair sliding back, and all but ran to the door where he paused long enough to turn around, blow out a couple of agitated breaths, and shake a finger at the moderator. "The whole school board is going to deal with this, Johnson! You countenance . . . backroom *treason*!"

The shouted last word and slamming door rang a numbness over them that defied any other sound for a moment, until finally Johnson ventured, "You may proceed, Mr. Farr."

Robert started again. "As I said, we are now at the heart of the problem. I want to thank all of you who are left, in advance, for hearing me out. I will certainly hear anything else you want to say to me when I am done in a few minutes.

"Also—about that thoughtless charge of 'backroom treason,' let me say that we are American citizens meeting in the conference room of a law office. I have a grievance against my government, and I fully intend to petition that government with my grievance according to the guidelines established *by* my government, unless you, my peers, can show that I'm wrong. It seems to me that this is the way things are *supposed* to be done in this country." He put his reading glasses on.

"Now—" Robert withdrew five paperback books from the manila envelope he had brought. "I have a copy of a little-known book for each of you. It's entitled, *Humanist Manifestos I and II*. I've underlined some relevant sentences in each book." He got up and placed a copy in front of each person, then returned to his seat. "Allow me to read the first sentence of the preface with my emphasis added: 'Humanism is a philosophical, *religious*, and moral point of view as old as human civilization itself.' Now, I read from the last paragraph, on page ten, of *Humanist Manifesto I* with my emphasis added: 'So stand the theses of *religious* humanism.'

"From beginning to end, humanism freely admits to being a religion. Let me read the first two affirmations of *Humanist Manifesto I*, found on page eight: 'First: Religious humanists regard the universe as self-existing and not created.

" 'Second: Humanism believes that man is a part of nature and that he has emerged as the result of a continuous process.'

"Finally, I'll read two sentences from *Humanist Mani-*

festo II, page sixteen: 'But we can discover no divine purpose or providence for the human species,' and 'No deity will save us; we must save ourselves.'

"These excerpts give the theme of humanism, that is: 'Man is the measure of all things.'" He took the glasses off and replaced them in his coat pocket.

Mayhew-Barr injected, "In all the time I've been in public education, I've never met anyone who said they were a humanist."

"Nor have I!" Connelly added. "There just isn't any such thing!"

Robert asked, "Have either of you ever heard of John Dewey?"

There was no immediate answer, but finally Mayhew-Barr said, "Of course."

"Do you agree that John Dewey had the greatest influence on education in the twentieth century?"

The principal nodded, and Connelly looked away.

"John Dewey was a board member of the American Humanist Association when that group produced *Humanist Manifesto I* in 1933. He was an atheist. The lack of discipline in the classroom and the belief that there are no absolute truths are just two of his contributions to our present educational methodology. In the nineteenth century, Horace Mann, another name familiar to educators, laid a great deal of the groundwork for the *religion* of humanism in our public schools.

"The point is: humanism *is* a religion—a very militant religion—which our government fully supports and propagates in the name of public education so that virtually every public educational building in this country is a temple for the worship of man. In fact, the Supreme Court ruled in 1961 that humanism *is* a religion! The religion of humanism is most definitely anti-Christian and anti-Bible. All of our media have fallen in line with what has been preached in our schools and universities until today Christians are beginning to be routinely persecuted and harassed."

Connelly stood with her book in her hand. "Excuse me," she said looking around at those seated. "Mr. Farr has had his say. I'm going to leave now because this fiasco has pointed up the necessity for a *real* meeting of the entire board! Let me say, Mr. Farr, that I'm going to read this book! I want you to know that Connelly goes on record as declaring herself a humanist here and now! Thank you, Mr. Farr, for once again so effectively pointing out the differences between foolishness and reason." She walked around the table, then the door closed softly.

Fred Stuart was gazing off into space while the two others who remained sat looking at Robert, who said, "That's all." He put a book back into the envelope and added, "For now."

Johnson cast a thoughtful glance at the ceiling and said, "It seems that we failed to make a full meeting unnecessary." To Robert he continued, "I believe what we heard and saw here bears out the thrust of what you have indicated, Mr. Farr. Mr. Stuart, do you have anything to say?"

"No. I'm going to need time to think through all this."

"Carol?"

"Nothing, except I'm disappointed that we couldn't prevent a meeting of the full board! Tell me, Robert—you said you're going to present a grievance to the government. What do you plan to do?"

"I plan to use letters, visits—any legitimate contacts to inform people so that we can raise a collective voice of protest against this violation of the First Amendment."

Stuart replied, "We're in for a big mess."

"We're already in a big mess," answered Robert. "And it goes far beyond the schools. When children are indoctrinated with evolution and given the responsibility for coming up with their own moral values, the stage is set for promiscuous sex, pornography, drugs, homosexuality, abortion, and rebellion. Even a strong family base is going to be unevenly matched against the influence of the schools and the media.

"And the phrase *separation of church and state* has been used in the wrong context for so long that very few people know that all it means is that the government doesn't belong in the religion business. Yet the federal government operates the world's largest religious subsidy. Now, I'm not proposing that we put religion in the business of government. What we need is for the government to get out of the religion business and return to the freedom of every person to practice his or her religion as the First Amendment guarantees."

When no one replied, Robert said, "I suppose the meeting is over and I'm free to go?"

"Yes," Johnson answered. "We'll all go."

They stood, and Robert exchanged a silent look with each of them, then he left the room, walking slowly down the darkened passage clutching the envelope. A wedge of light came from Cyrus Barr's office; he intended to pass by without looking in, but the man spoke his name so quietly that he wasn't sure he had. A glance at Barr's face as he sat at his desk confirmed the sound, and Robert went in.

The shirt-sleeved lawyer stood and extended his hand over the desk. "Cyrus Barr," he said.

"Robert Farr." Smiling, they shook hands.

"I take it," said Barr, "that whatever went on in there wasn't to everyone's satisfaction."

"You're right. I guess your wife mentioned what the meeting was all about."

"Nope." His smile increased to a near laugh. "You see, Carol and I have our own things to do."

"Oh—"

Now, the man did laugh. "Traditional, we are not! We're both, ah, very intelligent people, so there's no problem."

"Oh—well—" Robert could think of nothing to say, but the other man didn't seem to notice as he picked up a sport coat from the back of a chair. Barr jerked a thumb toward the desk stacked with forms, papers, folders, and pink memos. "Tomorrow's worries." He ran a hand down the back of his pepper-gray, neatly barbered head and said, "I'm here if you need me, whatever your problem. Except if it's psychiatric. I don't practice formal psychiatry, but I do refer—I know a couple of good shrinks! If you got problems, call us, that's why we're here. What line of work are you in, Farr?"

"I'm a fifth grade teacher. Your wife is my principal."

"Oh—okay! I guess that's logical! Well, as a teacher,

you probably should retain our whole firm!" He laughed again and ended with a tentative smile. "Seriously—I'm here. And, on a teacher's salary, I know you might be hesitant. But don't be."

"Thanks. I'll keep that in mind."

"Walk you to your car?"

"Okay. Could you tell me what line of work Mr. Allen Johnson is in?"

"Dr. Johnson? Obstetrics and gynecology. He's a top-notch doctor, but he won't do abortions."

"Do you think that's bad?"

"It is when your fifteen-year-old daughter needs one! We had to go with an unknown—but everything turned out okay."

Just then Barr looked past Robert to the door and said, "Here's the good doctor now, and some lawyer's wife!" She stepped into the office, and her husband moved over and gave her a peck on the cheek.

"Robert," she said, turning to him, "Dr. Johnson has just been paged, and he needs to get back to the hospital. But he wants to ask Cyrus a question. Would you excuse us?"

"Surely." After a momentary exchange of politeness with Carol and her husband, he shook hands with Dr. Johnson in the doorway and nodded when he said, "We'll be in touch, Mr. Farr."

Robert continued to the brightly lighted reception area. The woman was gone: everyone, it seemed, was gone, and typewriters and computers rested in silence under beige or gray dustcovers. Nobody. He thought about the pictures in the coldness of pink snow and the chalet leaning upslope against a mountain with nobody there to see. Perhaps they were all inside. Yes, they were all inside and talking, and outside there was nobody to see, nobody to know.

Outside the building, he stood in the gathering darkness and looked down Mayhew Street. The streetlights had come on, and far down the way, a lone someone was walking under one.

6

There had been a Saturday like this before, long ago and, as the boy had said, far, far away. A time when everything was good and his father was there with the sun on his face, and his hands and his smile worked in tandem.

Robert watched them sleeping, each child unborn as it were from his or her bed and from their rooms. Standing between those rooms, almost at the same time he could watch them, but not quite—as he and Paula used to do in another place and at other times. Especially Christmases.

Rooms and halls and standing watching. Down streets and out windows. From behind sandbags. And on the sand. With the tide running and the wind and waves from the horizon coming in and her standing there in her strong silence for him and him only. He wanted her more with every look, and when he kept looking, her head and eyelids dropped in her pleasure at being his wife. He was trying to distract himself by looking at the horizon because she had wanted to come here to watch the waves. And then she told him, her voice mixing with the breeze and her fragrance. He wept and hurt her with his arms so that she couldn't breathe until he remembered to release her. Both times she had used the beach to tell him.

He wanted her now as much as ever. The aching inside grew worse whenever he remembered her standing beside him, so he would try not to—like the time he had looked at the horizon and tried to think that she wasn't there, but it hurt too much, so he had given it up just before she told him. If only he had known—

Paula would be surprised at how much Michael and Penny had grown in five years. At times they seemed not to remember her. Then he would tell them again how she would laugh with her eyes because of them, but they wouldn't know because they didn't know how to read eyes—then.

Now they were sleeping and still not knowing, in their innocence, so many things. Like that it was Saturday and how a Saturday had happened before with the sun coming up and how his father had stood and watched him sleeping. Robert knew now that he must have.

They would be excited when he awakened them, not only because of the horses but because of her—Beatrice—the one Penny had called pretty—twice—and looked at him to see what he would do. And he had said yes both times, nodding his head. The children had glanced at each other like something bad was coming to an end, and he had pretended again not to see. But he had seen. Finally.

It was like the beach, out there by himself—walloped

by a wave he had seen but forgotten, rolled over the sandy bottom, feeling the wave's power as though it were a giant child that would finally let him breathe when it remembered. She was so much more than pretty. And it hadn't been a week, yet it seemed he had always known her—from just that night, behind him there in the kitchen five days ago and every day since at lunch. And last night in what he had called the living room but knew now that until last night it had not been. When she had come over, they sat talking about the meeting, and Robert had been afraid—a grown man, trembling inside that Beatrice might see or hear some hint of the war going on inside him for her.

Robert knew that he had tried to fool himself by fleeting the word *war* through his mind; there was no war; it was no contest. Every reason to resist her had turned tail and run; every excuse had gone over. She was no enemy, definitely no enemy, and now Robert the boy and Robert the man were scared. And totally confused. Because some of all this was swirling around not only Beatrice, but . . . Carol Mayhew-Barr.

And that was wrong and crazy. Because she was an enemy. Maybe not as much as before, because she had seen to it that Johnson moderated the meeting. Carol had at least made his battle something like fair. He would probably be fired, yet she appeared to be trying to help him. *But the woman is married.* The woman is married.

Definitely it was Beatrice who stood beside him strong in his mind, and it was Beatrice that he was most afraid of because she was *not* an enemy, and his fear was that she would know. Yet, he could think of no reason for her not to know except something called time.

Last night when he told what the principal had done to get Johnson to moderate, he said Carol's name as he had said it that day in her office, and he hadn't meant to, either time. It was as if Beatrice had not heard, but she had and there was understanding in her eyes. In that moment Robert knew her strength, and he turned away lest she see too much.

Shadley Academy read the green and gold pennant on the wall over Michael's bed beside the window. Home of the Shamrocks. Natasha's green triangular girl came to mind, and he turned to Penny sleeping with her arm around her teddy bear and her blonde hair swirled over her shoulder and under her chin. It was hard for him to do her hair for a long time; the barrettes wouldn't stay in place. She would come home from school looking better than when she left, and when he asked, she said her teacher would do her hair and not say anything. She needed a mother and so did Michael.

The sun was coming in Michael's window; but it was still too early to wake them, so Robert turned and started back to the kitchen for another cup of coffee. He stopped at the door of his room to stare at the bed with the covers awry and the imprint of where he had lain, sometimes sleeping but mostly trying to. He was as excited as Michael and Penny but for very different reasons. This would be a day—no matter how it turned out—that the three of them would never forget. And he hoped she wouldn't either.

As Robert sat at the table and drank his coffee alone

that morning, he could see, finally he knew: Michael and Penny needed a mother. And it hadn't even been a week.

The house was a big, old farmhouse, the kind you look at and imagine you grew up in. Robert thought, without wondering why, about how it would have been to be her brother and wake up every morning in his bedroom with its high ceiling of narrow, tongue-in-groove cream-colored wood. The walls were papered with faded roses on trellises yellowed by time and the sun so that the room itself seemed to be receding into the grayish mist of a long forgotten morning. An old baseball glove lay on the dresser, and a bubble gum card of Switch-hitting Mick was stuck on the mirror. They were from the early days. Otherwise, she said, everything was just the way her parents said Daniel left it. Beatrice turned away, beautiful even in jeans and a denim jacket. "I remember *him*," she said, "but not so much the room, because the room is always here."

When she said that, she was looking in the dresser mirror, but he knew she didn't see it. He wanted to hold her then more than he had wanted to hold on to anyone for five years and remember it all . . . all the green velvet spread out below, humped and cut up by rivers . . . the throbbing roar of the chopper's blades and the blue infinity overhead . . . chest-high grass waving out like a silvered green ocean from the downwash. Scrambling out the door, guys running, shooting . . . falling . . . dying . . . his guys. After he had remembered it all, they would open their eyes and it never happened. He and Daniel would shake hands right here. Robert wanted to hold her and do that for her.

Her parents were gone for the weekend, and she didn't come upstairs much anymore. She would ride on Saturdays and during the summer, sometimes every day. There were miles of dirt roads around and plenty of fields and even some fences to jump. And yes, once in a while she rode at night, and yes, she often saw deer and even knew where some of them bedded. And yes, she was ready to go riding right now, and sure, Michael could ride Sugar, and Penny, Spice.

Down at the barn, sunshine came slanting in bars through weather-beaten boards, and the smell of hay, horses, and leather permeated the dimness that gradually gave up its secrets as their eyes adjusted. Beatrice was straightening a bridle in her hands when her face and hair came full into a splash of light so golden and soft that it traced the brownness of her eyes, leaving little flecks of itself sparkling around the warmth of all he had ever known.

In that moment of gold glimmering upon her head, she smiled as if she were a gift given to him as life had been given to him and she did not know. The soft smoothness of her skin he could feel without touching because of the light answering light from her face. Her teeth glistened like snow, and her hair was the color of honey maple. She smiled again, seeing, he was sure, only the brilliance of the sun, but she was looking toward him, trusting that he was there yet not knowing. And in that, too—she was so beautiful.

In a few moments the bridle was on a horse, and she led them to the doorway and the sun, where its warmth could be inhaled while the coolness of the barn lingered a heartbeat or two before departing from his lumberjack shirt and jeans. Michael and Penny explored the horse's neck with their hands as high as they could reach until Spice's head came down to theirs, and there were hugs, nuzzles, and laughter.

Robert stood back watching. It seemed that her movements were all predetermined, leaving her eyes free to see only the children and to make her excitement that of a little girl about to embark on a great adventure. The saddle was on, a western one with a horn to hold on to, and she looked once over her shoulder—more than a glance—at him, and there was nothing of the look she had when Allen had said he would solve the puzzle. There was something in that look that he had not seen in a long time, something needed and precious in its rarity; it was a look of knowing.

She adjusted the stirrups upward, told Penny to hold Spice's bridle and rub her muzzle until she came back with Sugar. "She's a very gentle horse," she said to Robert, "and used to children."

"Used to children?" he asked.

"Yes. I love children," she said simply, pausing before the darkness of the barn. "So— I go and get some of the more unloved ones sometimes and bring out here for the day."

He and Michael followed her into the barn. "Have you decided about being a teacher yet?" Robert said to her back.

"Of course."

"Of course, what?"

"Robert—don't you know?" She was sliding a wooden bar out with a bridle ready in the other hand.

"No. You see, it's not been a good week for being a teacher—well, a certain kind of teacher."

"Robert," she said with a suddenly hushed voice, "would you come here?"

He walked to where she and Michael were standing beside the horse's feed trough. A beam of sunlight was sloping down into the trough onto a little impression in the hay, bathing it in gold. She said softly, "There's never been a good time for a certain kind . . . of teacher."

His hand touched hers, and then he held it tightly. Several moments later he released it and walked quickly toward the door.

"What's wrong?" asked Michael's voice behind him.

"Nothing," came her muffled reply, "nothing's wrong—"

"Why are you crying, Miss Beatrice?"

"I'm happy—that's all, I'm just happy."

Robert stood outside in the sun, looking away at the house reaching into the unbounded blueness of the sky with grass and brown earth rambling as far as he could see. His fingers clutched the compass in his pocket. Behind him the children were asking questions, and she was laughing again. Leather squeaked as a cinch was pulled tight. In a moment, he would need to turn around, and he would. He would face them and look at them, and they would all laugh together. But it would not be like before. Now, he was happy. That's all . . . just happy.

◘

The children were asleep on an old, patchwork quilt in a darkened corner of the den. A solitary lamp stood in the opposite corner behind the couch that fronted the fireplace where the slow-dancing flames of gas logs provided the only other light in the house. It might have been the large brown and beige oval rug surrounding them, or the beige tiled floor beyond that, or the heavy oak mantle over the stone fireplace, but somehow the grays of the barren trees and the brown of the fields—everything in that incredible sun-filled day—seemed to be undiminished here in the room and in the darkness beyond.

Robert sat gazing at the flames with the day reliving itself, it seemed, in all his senses like laying awake for those moments before sleep after a day at the beach, rising and dipping with the rolling waves, seeing again the smooth carpet of sand and knowing the feel of the wind. The walking, riding, and much more walking, following the children and laughing at so much . . . at how the horses obeyed her voice rather than their small riders.

Finally, they had had their fill of riding, and with the sandwiches Beatrice had provided long gone, Michael and Penny—all of them—admitted that they were hungry. It was getting dark, and they were a long way from the barn, he thought, and so did the kids. Yet just over the next rise, there they were: the shadowed silhouettes of the house and barn against a fiery sunset.

It wasn't long before they were eating in the dining room that Beatrice had prepared as for formal guests. Michael and Penny were sleepy even before the table was cleared, so she had spread the quilt. She had done so much that day.

He felt her fingers soft on the back of his hand. He did not move as every sensation and thought fled away except for her touch. A great, silent wind began to stir from long ago; it could not be felt, for it was a long way off, yet it could be known.

But the knowing made a great and mighty dread. Robert struggled with the inner wind, making again his blinded way as a man might throw himself against a tree to hold on in the face of a hurricane. Paula was in her coffin, in his mind as he last saw her. As if asleep under the cold and silent earth with her hands folded . . . the ring on her finger in the awful darkness of silence, the black silence of midnight under the earth.

Tell me about her. How? What can I say? She's gone to a place that we can't know—here. Robert? We can't know—

"Robert?"

He turned with widened eyes to the woman beside him. Beatrice must have been saying—"Did you say something?"

"Tell me about her."

"Who?"

"Your wife."

He studied the floor, the patterns in the brown and beige oval rug, the lines of the tiles. Her fingers moved, and she was holding his hand as tightly as he had held hers. He looked at her eyes glistening in the shadows. "I loved her, and—" Possibly a minute passed before he dropped his head and added softly, "I killed her."

Now both of her hands were holding his, but she said nothing.

"Now, you know."

"I know nothing, Robert. Tell me."

He hesitated and then said, "We were going to a PTO meeting, just her and me. I was driving, and it was at night and raining. A drunk came at us head-on. I swerved the wrong way, and Paula took the impact."

"Robert—" There was a pause. "Do you really believe Paula's death was your fault?"

"I could have taken the impact."

"If you could do it again, would you?"

"Yes."

"I know you would." Beatrice turned her head and looked at the fireplace for some time. He did, too, until she said, "Do you know why you're grieving?"

He met her eyes and answered, "I know why."

"I don't think so. Paula is gone, and you sorrow over that. But there's something else that bothers you a lot more."

"What's that?"

"You deeply regret the fact that you're not God. If you had known what was going to happen, you would have avoided it, or changed it, wouldn't you?"

"Yes."

"Well, you *didn't* know. So you did what you could in an instant with no time to make an informed decision. What you're really sorry for is that it wasn't your call. If it had been, you think you could have made a better one. We *cannot* know that."

Robert looked away with no reply.

"Let God be God."

He paused and then asked, "Where did you come up with this?"

"It's taught throughout the Bible."

"I know that."

"And, then too—"

"What?"

"I've been praying *your* prayer, Robert."

He wanted to laugh but felt like crying. Then he did venture a kind of trial laugh. "Yeah—" His gaze dropped from her face to the couch between them where their hands were joined. He squeezed hers, and she squeezed back.

Indecision held him fast as he beheld her from under what he felt was a furrowing brow. *We don't know each other,* he was thinking and almost said. *How much do we have to know?* he asked himself.

The inner wind pushed memories from before, or fragments of what might have been so called. One day . . . today? Or would he retreat forever before dead leaves scratching and clattering over muddy ice kept from the sun by the shadows of dead trees standing into blue infinity? Death as a way of life? Fragments lifeless in their scurrying before the wind. The compass—what had the boy seen in his father? "What was his name?" Robert asked, turning now to words.

"Whose name?"

"The man you would have married."

"His name? His name was Bob."

The flames were blue inside with gold edges. They danced before him now instead of her face. *Whose name?* Someone she would have married . . . whose name . . . would have been hers . . . except . . .

Michael and Penny were sleeping soundly on the old quilt. Not knowing that as they slept, their father—

He released her hands and memorized her face. Flecked again with misty gold, her eyes held the warmth of all he had ever known. He barely whispered, "Bob—did not make a mistake."

The firelight made two little golden lines of tears tracing down her face. Slowly, he raised his hands and brushed at them with his fingers. Her hand was soft as warm silk on his face as she did the same. Then he was holding her and feeling the strength of her arms around him and her breathing, or her trying to, and her softness, the softness he needed to press into his chest to make it part of himself. An incredible emptiness was becoming no more, and she was filling it with her lips on his for more than a moment. Then she was touching his face again with her fingers and trying to move back. Robert would not let her, but she was gently shaking her head and whispering, "No." He wanted her more than a man could want anything, and he tried to remember the horizon of unknowingness, but all he could see was her in this day and in the duskiness before him and the impossibility of her word.

One of the children stirred, and he began to release her. It was this, too, that he had been afraid of. But there was no fear or remorse in her eyes as she raised his hand to her face and moved back a little more and then kissed that hand. With no words she sat like this for some time holding his hand to her face with her eyes closed and her lips all but moving. The picture of her and of the children beyond, he drank in, not only with his eyes but with that part of himself he had thought dead and buried. And though he could not close his eyes to her, he was borne upward again on a swelling wave of thankfulness.

As he moved toward her, she released his hand and abruptly stood. He sat breathing and trying to look at the darkness across the room without seeing it as darkness but as a gathering dawn. His eyes would come back always to the children asleep. He remembered how well she had handled the horses, so why not—he was realizing the humor now—him?

Beatrice was beside the children, standing there watching them sleep. Thinking about how it seemed that she had always been a part of this family and weighing that against the void of the past five years, he realized that she would not simply fill that void, she would dispel it as though it had never been. He would remember it, he was sure, but it would be no more.

As he thought of that, he could remain alone no longer; he got up and went to stand beside her. There were no words as their fingers met and interlocked, and Robert remembered the beginning, so long ago, of this day and his watching Michael and Penny as they slept. Now as they stood there together, he looked at Beatrice and recalled again the beach and the same wanting even as he had once wanted Paula—always—in his life. Lifting his eyes to the darkened far wall, he tried the horizon, but again it didn't work. With his free right hand he fingered the compass in his pocket and wondered anew what the boy had seen about his father that had prompted this gift. Dropping his gaze . . . their breathing was so peaceful. He released Beatrice's hand and put his arm around her and drew her tightly to his side.

As much as the day before had been bound only by receding horizons and a sky unfettered of clouds, the next came contained largely in the confines of the stone house. Not that the small place served in any way to restrict them—it did not—but it seemed that the sun of yesterday had actually come into its coolness with them and warmed it immediately, suffusing also every nook and corner with a light not known—ever—in the rooms and halls and even the closets as they hung up their Sunday coats. Blinds were flung open by whoever was nearest the particular window in question; and first Penny, then Michael went about pulling the double cords to the right of each window long and hard so that the slats collected themselves upward in a succession of quick clatters. They were raising sails, it seemed, and ringing bells. For she was here with them in the house.

They had gone to church together. And together they

had sung, standing there in the third pew of the tiny building, singing as none of the little congregation had ever heard the Farrs sing. Everybody just had to meet her, and there were hopeful smiles and laughter and even some dabbing at eyes by a couple of the older ladies. Beatrice's easy smile belonged there, an old man told her while Michael gazed up in apparent wonder at his hearing aid and wrinkles as if he had never before seen Mr. Swenson, his Sunday School teacher for the last three years.

A meal came into being under her hands. She talked as she worked, not needing more than two tries to find whatever she needed, asking only one question, that concerning the whereabouts of the bread pan. It was, he told her, in the cabinet under the sink, catching water from a leak in the trap. After all, it was only a very slow leak, and by using a wide pan, the water would evaporate and not need emptying. Besides, he didn't make bread anyway.

Beatrice was stooped way down, nearly sitting on her heels, the cabinet door open and her looking in, when she raised her hands to the sink and rested her head between them, her shoulders shaking. As Robert started toward her, she dropped to her knees in laughter, turned sideways, and flopped back on her seat to lean against the cabinet, laughing uncontrollably so that her narrowed eyes released more than a few tears that she wiped at before covering her face with her hands. Then she peeked up at him standing there and slid just a little further down in her paroxysm of hilarity, beauty, and utter aliveness.

In a few moments she lay at his feet with her hands gone from her face, looking up at him with her sweater and skirt slightly awry and her wet face flushed with merriment. "It evaporates," she said, and again it came upon her, this humor that gladdened his heart too much for anything other than looking. It was then that he knew. It was now that he would have to tell her.

Robert knelt and ran the back of his fingers up her cheek. She took his hand and held it to her face, her eyes shining. With his other hand he took her hand away, and he saw the question in her eyes. Gently, he put an arm beneath her back and a hand under her knees and slowly stood. They were rising, both of them it seemed, far above the house and all the things in it and in the world. Her face was all he could see; all else receded and was gone. Except Beatrice, God's gift to him as life was His gift.

Far above the earth he could have looked down and the green velvet lumped and cut up by rivers might have spread out below him. But there was no sound and no jungle. "I love you," he said, and there were more tears on her face.

Her lips moved and her whispered words came. "I've always loved you, Robert. As long ago as I can remember. Before I knew you, I loved you."

He released her legs, and her feet went lightly to the floor. He held her as tightly as he dared with his eyes closed into the fragrance of her hair and the strength of her arms squeezing air from his lungs. There was no barren tree and no jungle. There was no more aching inside—only their arms holding on to each other.

From somewhere behind him Michael and Penny were saying something, then there was quiet. He opened his eyes to the sink and the open cabinet door. The bread pan sat out of recessed shadows as if it had been in the oven and they were just in from church with his mother taking it out while still wearing the dress that was black in the house and blue in the sun, the one covered with white dots. He had been no taller than the top of the oven door when it was closed; that was the pan, and he could never have known then that one day . . .

"Hey, Dad—aren't you hungry?" chimed the boy's voice behind him.

His sister hissed, "Shh!"

"Well, we changed clothes like Dad said! And even hung up the others, too!"

"Would you shut up!" the girl whispered emphatically.

Beatrice's explosive little giggle was nearly muffled by his collar and without changing their position, he pivoted her around so he could see them standing in the doorway. "Yes," he said into her hair, "I'm hungry. But I was telling this lady why the bread pan is under the sink." Robert let her go, and as she turned to them, he made a little gesture as if to present her. "Lady and gentleman—" He paused so as to remember their faces standing there in the doorway looking up at her as they had the first time. They couldn't know—could they?—what was coming next. *He* had not known; he had not planned this; it was all just happening right here in the kitchen, and—well—"Michael, Penny . . . would you please come here?"

They did, and their faces, he thought, had a certain solemn expectation as he knelt to their level. "I believe—" he began, suddenly not knowing exactly what to say. Penny's eyes were getting misty, and maybe his were, too.

"I believe both of you like Miss Beatrice a whole lot, don't you?"

They nodded vigorously, and the boy said, "Yes, sir."

"Well, I like her a lot too. In fact, I love her."

Robert brushed, clumsily he felt, at the eyes of both children and then hugged them together for a few heartbeats of wet faces. He stood them back where they were and said, "So—" Robert looked up into Beatrice's face. "I'm asking this woman to be my wife—and I'm asking her to be . . . your mother."

Beatrice was with them on her knees, and out of the jumble of heads and hair and tears and arms she was saying, "Yes! Yes!" and Robert was thinking that he had done it again: for the second time he had asked a woman to marry him, and she had said yes to a very uncertain future.

The time with Paula came to his mind, a time when the children's names were words and sounds with no meanings that he could know then. She had waited with bowed head and closed eyes before saying yes. Yes on the steps of a Sunday morning park gazebo. Yes just before church; she always insisted on church.

Michael hugged Beatrice, laughing away tears. *Michael Robert*, Paula said when she held him the first time. *Michael* to remember the angel's name who will shout when Jesus takes his people out of a hostile world. *Penny* he named the little girl also clutching Beatrice's neck and looking at him with shining eyes . . . in the hope that he would always have one. But now—maybe he wouldn't. One day she would probably say her own *yes*, and he would give her up. But, for some reason, that was no longer such a bad thought.

When they got up from their knees, still wiping their faces and laughing, they kept on touching her—the children did—almost holding on, wanting, it seemed, to stay close while not being a bother. Beatrice went back to preparing lunch as if it were the most natural thing in the world to get up from the floor engaged to a family she had not known two weeks before. Robert sat down at the table and watched, which seemed the thing to do, especially to see if the kids would set the table as usual. They did, and the boy said something under his breath as he placed the silverware, something like, "Way to go, Dad!"

Robert fingered the compass in his pocket and thought his one-word prayer. As the clatter and chatter was going on, Beatrice paused at the stove and looked at him as she had yesterday over her shoulder, more than a glance. A little while later Robert was still pondering the table top and trying in vain to remember a time when he had been happier.

"Robert," said Carol Mayhew-Barr, leaning against his desk again, "this whole mess is getting deeper and deeper. Dr. Johnson says he sees sense in what you said the other day and agrees fully. He's a very cautious person, but he's extremely thorough. Franklin is as riled up as anyone has ever seen him, and he's known to be a loose cannon! I think he probably has a couple of board members swayed already, and they could well be coming after *me* because he apparently saw through the situation with Dr. Johnson moderating the meeting! Superintendent Spivey, of course, is a politician, so he stalled and cooled Franklin down a little when he stormed into his office the other day, but at least Franklin made an appointment—"

He was still facing partly away from her, not having moved since her entrance into the room less than a minute ago. A slow, deliberate turn carouselled the empty classroom into a panorama designed to be remembered as one of his last. Stopping, his eyes found her face, rose to the date he had written on the board—Wednesday, March 1, 1989—and then went easily back to her. "Good morning," Robert said.

"Good morning."

"I'm sorry."

"So am I, Robert. So am I."

"What do you want me to do?"

"What do *I* . . . want you to do?"

"Yes. I don't want to make trouble for you."

"Are you willing to back down?"

"No. But I am willing to do what I can not to hurt you."

"Not hurt me?"

"Yes. You asked me not to, remember?"

"Oh! That—" She laughed and said, shaking her head, "You *are* a typical man!"

"What do you mean?"

Her humor had become a diminutive smile. "Nothing."

"Yes, you do." The words had come without thought, and regret followed with the big breath he took, looking away.

"What do *you* mean?"

"You do mean something."

"Tell me about it, Robert."

Meeting her eyes, he replied, "Everyone means something. No one's life should be wasted."

"Do you think mine is being wasted?"

"Lost more than wasted."

"Am I losing—my life?"

"Every day."

"I told you, Robert—I *don't* lose."

A pause came while he gazed at her and tried to collect his thoughts. The two actions seemed incompatible, so he focused out the window. "What about Connelly, Franklin, and the board? You said some of them might be after you. Doesn't that concern you?"

"Robert—look at me." He did, and she came away from the desk to stand upright. "I love a good fight! Franklin and his crowd are a bunch of turkeys! Connelly's a wimp, and I told her so to her face Monday morning! She didn't part her lips, but I think she's sneaked in somewhere and heard one of our private conversations. Maybe she's outside listening to this one—well, she can get an ear full of this! The whole board can come after me! They've got nothing! We'll start talking foreclosures on certain businesses, stores, land, and houses—just for starters! If they want to play in the dirt, I've got plenty! We can talk about certain embarrassing business deals, or a certain trip last year that ended up in a motel room for one of our own—instead of the statewide teachers' conference! I know how 'sick' our darling teacher was, and I know who the 'doctor' was who made a 'house call' to that motel! And I know where *she* teaches, and her reputation— How do you think the wimp would like them apples, Robert?"

Something like a transparent impression, lasting no more than a couple of seconds, sprang full-blown to his mind before being snatched away as if before a mighty wind. He had remembered a wood chip he had made into a ship by sticking a hickory leaf into its splintered end for a sail. The creek was rain swollen, and he had gotten his best shoes muddy to launch it eventually to the sea where it finally would be free even if he could not be free from their arguing and silences. The chip and leaf were blasted apart by the water in its whiteness to disappear in the muddy brown of stinging tears. No more than two seconds. Carried along by the onrush like the chip. "I'm sorry," he said again, feeling a nauseous spasm in his guts for Connelly—sick and sorry for everything Carol had called "this whole mess."

"Up until Friday," she was saying, "I pretty well had things contained. But now—" Her face went floorward, providing a visual echo of the word *mess*. "Now," she repeated to the floor, "things have gotten slightly out of hand." Her eyes locked onto his, and her face did not raise. "Connelly did her homework well! A couple of significant people, as she called them, have bought into her accusations that you're a child molester."

Stomach-pit sickening returned intensified with a numb, ringing silence like a hall bell.

"What's more," she continued, "Franklin has called a couple of state people. It may not be contained anymore, Robert—"

"Why?" he asked louder than necessary. Dropping his voice, he repeated, "Why? Why are they doing this to me?"

"That's what I want to know."

Robert paused, trying to make sense of her words. "What do you mean, that's what you want to know? You yourself called me stupid, you said my faith was dead, you said—"

"Forget that!"

"Why should I forget the very reason all these things are happening? What you said is what they believe. Why should—"

"What I said is not important. Why should you ask why? You've answered your own question about why you're being singled out. And something else, Robert. Do you believe in what you're doing? Do you believe that what you said in the meeting is absolutely true?"

"Yes! Of course I believe it's true! Why else would I—"

"Then stop telling me you're sorry!"

"I mean—I'm sorry that I'm causing trouble for you."

"Yeah? Well, don't be!" She turned quickly and walked to the door where she looked up and down the hall before returning to where she was before. Carol gave him a sizing-up look and nodded at a student's desk. "Sit down," she said. "Let's both of us sit down. We've got time, and I want us to talk." They squeezed into two students' desks side by side.

Robert's mind took a picture of her sitting there looking up at the chalkboard for that moment in the undersized desk, collecting *her* thoughts and blowing *his* mind. She turned to face him as he tried to focus between her eyebrows and tell himself that she wasn't beautiful. "Robert—" His name was said as if a great adventure was about to be embarked on. A theme park on a ride with so many laughing children in the empty seats behind them, and they were all children and excited and yet a little scared, but the grown-ups were somewhere near, so everything was all right. It was going to be all right, so . . . hold on, Robert . . . for the children. They were moving now . . . for she had said his name, and her woman's word, and her woman's face—for the barest instant—had been a child's. No, they *were* children, now, and moving on the strength of her faraway gaze out the window behind him.

"All my life—I've seen power. Power over people's lives and people's futures . . . power motivated by greed. My father has power over the entire school board. Most of them, he could—and probably will—crush. My husband—" Her eyes came again to Robert's to plunge in deeply with a look of heavy longing. "My husband—if I can call him that—Cyrus has the wherewithal and know-how to manipulate the Wardensville scales of justice virtually any way he wants. And he will do what I ask. But now I'm not so sure anymore, I'm just not so sure."

"Not so sure about what?"

"You see, Robert, I'm a fair-minded person. And, well— You see, I've talked with Dr. Johnson, and he's . . . a scientist, a doctor. And he believes—"

"He believes what?"

"Like you do."

"So?"

"So—" She was gazing past him again. "So I don't know. Look—" A glance bounced from him to linger somewhere outside. "I have a question, but first I want to say something. I want to say that, eventually, some state people may be getting into our affairs. Now that doesn't scare me. But I can't control what those people do. This could turn out to be a real battle, but still, ultimately, they can't really hurt me even if they were to pull my certification, which is highly improbable.

"But . . ." She looked at him. "That's not the case with you, Robert. You stand to lose everything. Remember, I've been in education a long time. I turned down Spivey's job because I just want to run a school. That's all I've ever wanted to do. But the educational field is a jungle! On most levels, whatever gets you ahead is what you do, and fair is a big carnival with rides and shows that comes in October."

"Why have you always wanted to run a school?"

"I don't know why, and I don't really care anymore. But you stand to lose everything. I've watched you and listened to you. I've talked with Dr. Johnson about the meeting. I don't know what makes people like the two of you tick, and that bothers me! You stand to gain nothing; you stand to lose everything. Robert—why?"

"It's right."

"What *is* right and wrong anymore? How can you possibly *know* that you're right?"

"Carol, look at it like a child. Can you do that?"

She raised her head, and her face wore a questioning look.

"Sure you can. You do it every day in this place."

"But we *aren't* children."

"Aren't we? Honestly, Carol—do you believe that? What happened to the little girl you were? Wasn't it she who wanted to sit in that little desk . . . again? Isn't she the one who always wanted to run a school? Wasn't it children who went to the moon because they had always wanted to go there?"

She glanced away. "We grow up. Somebody in your Bible said something about leaving childish things behind."

"That was Paul. Childish, yes. Child*like*, no. Jesus said that whoever would not receive the kingdom of God—or the rule of God—as a little child could not enter it, or ever get into heaven."

"Heaven—" Carol echoed with another faraway look. Then she shook her head and said, "Here's my question: If God is good, why does He allow evil in the world?"

After a pause, Robert replied, "When I was in Vietnam, a general was riding in a helicopter high above a battle going on in a clearing in the jungle. The general asked the pilot to take him down so he could see the battle. The pilot obliged by going down and flying between the Cong and Americans while Charlie threw everything he had at that chopper: automatic weapons fire, rockets, grenades, the works. For some reason the chopper wasn't hit, and when it landed the pilot was hauled into headquarters and asked why he had put the general in such danger. He said, 'The general said he wanted to see the battle, so I took him to where he could see.'

"Carol, when Adam and Eve ate the fruit of the knowledge of good and evil, they were fully aware of what the word *knowledge* meant. It was the same word used for sexual intercourse. The word meant 'to be intimately involved with.' So Adam and Eve said, in effect, 'We want to be intimately involved with evil and know it fully.' All they

had ever known was good, but by their actions they specifi-
cally *asked* to see and experience evil on an intimate basis.
God obliged them and us because he takes the human race
very seriously."

The woman looked at him with doubtful eyes. "But
Adam and Eve weren't real."

"Do you think the results of their actions are real?"

Her gaze returned to the window. At length she said,
"I'm going to help you all I can in this situation, Robert.
But—"

"You said that there might be a big battle. If it comes,
there's going to be some evil. Do you want to see it and be
in it?"

"Of course I do!"

"See? That's why God allows evil in His world."

She smiled. "I see . . . and I want to see, and I want to
know . . . a *lot* of things."

Now he looked up at the chalkboard. In a moment
Carol freed herself from the desk and got up. Robert
stood, and she moved even closer to him. "I want you to
know . . . that you've gotten me . . . thinking. I want us to
get together again and talk. We could be closer than you
think."

"Carol, this is part of the battle, part of the war. It's not
just coming; it's here. It's always been here—it's *inside* us."

"And, as I recall, you're afraid of those passions."

"Yes, I am. And there's something else you need to
know."

"What else do I need to know, Robert?"

"I'm engaged."

Her eyes flared as she recoiled backward. "What? Engaged? You—" Her hand swept across her forehead. "Engaged—who?"

"Beatrice Bertram."

"But—but she's just an aide, and—" Her sentence died amid her clenched eyes and shaking head. The look she finally gave him came through eyes that spilled little streams down her face. "Go on!" she blurted, "go on and be engaged! She can't help you! Go on, you simpleminded bumpkin! You're on your own! You've got nothing, no chance!" The woman spun around and ran to the door. "I hope they crucify you!"

The noise of pounding heels echoing and reechoing as she ran down the hall filled the blackness of his closed eyes. Robert's head dropped, and he was holding on to the back of the little desk with all his strength.

8

To lean on the little desk was awkward, and to hold it so tightly made his arms ache. Yet Robert did not immediately release it, nor did he straighten up right away. Instead, he stood as he was until the awkwardness and aching became uppermost in his mind and the essence of knowing had to do with when not to bow to the past. And how time can make mud into stone, and mighty sailing ships into splinters, and splinters into muddy memories.

He let go of the desk, straightened up, and opened his eyes into those of Beatrice standing in the doorway. Nothing came to mind to say; she had seen and heard something— what he did not know. Wood chips and splintered ships knew nothing. They are simply borne along in their simple-minded, bumpkin way.

"What happened?" came her voice, too even against the doorway's last tempest.

What does it matter? he wanted to say, but could

not—not to her, even though she seemed like a stranger, complete in her strangeness standing there saying, *Tell me about it, Robert,* because he had said she meant something when she said nothing, or was it the other way around? "Nothing," he replied, "nothing at all."

She came into the room, and he watched her walking slowly, carrying a shoe box and a composition book, one of those hardbacked black ones flecked with little white splotches that had once been white dots that had all burst and turned to stringy, amoeba-shaped nothings. It would be black inside or outside the house except for the nothings on an old dress leaning down before a flat pan stuck out of the shadows of an old, long gone oven.

Connelly had listened outside a door once or more. Why not Beatrice Bertram? Why not everybody—the school board, the world—everybody in the world trying to cram it down his throat that he was wrong, a simpleminded bumpkin. The two words were forming loudly on his lips to tell her to get out—and never come back. To never come back—nothing—nothing could ever come back. *Get out*—the air for shouting was rushing up from his guts when she stopped behind his desk and looked at the floor, and he saw her pain. She was looking at his silence laying back there on the floor behind his desk as if she could read it, as if she understood what he could never say and why his silence was pushed back there out of the way like the rotting corpse of a dead schoolchild. The anger on her face stopped him.

"I'm supposed to work in the library today," she hollowly said without ceasing to stare at the floor. "So I came in the back door. I was walking up the hall when I heard

Carol say she hoped they would crucify you. She ran out of the room and down the hall. She never saw me."

Robert stood listening to the silence and watching anger slowly harden her face. Beatrice turned unhurriedly and walked back to the door, where she paused before facing him. Her face was no longer hard, and her voice was soft as she said, "Robert, I'm praying for you." Then she was gone, swallowed, it seemed, by the silence of all that had happened.

That afternoon after school, Robert was sitting in the waiting room of Dr. Allen Johnson's OB/GYN suite. The women there, most of them pregnant, would eye him from time to time with something akin to mild interest—or perhaps it was disinterest. At any rate, he was here because Dr. Johnson himself had called the school—at recess—and asked him to come. The doctor had arranged his schedule so that his associates would see patients between four and four-thirty.

At exactly four o'clock, Robert was called and led by the receptionist to a small office with no windows, two chairs in addition to the one behind the desk, and a Monet painting of haystacks on the wall. "It's an original," Robert said following the greeting, sure that it was but adding for politeness, "isn't it?"

"Yes," the doctor replied, dismissing the receptionist with a nod. She closed the door, and Dr. Johnson came around the desk and sat down next to Robert after he had been seated. "Thanks for coming, Mr. Farr. Our time is limited and, because of the meeting the other day, there are several areas I want to go over. This preliminary discussion is to help determine what course of action might be indicated.

"Mr. Farr, I have long been an observer of a very dangerous trend in the federal government. Our government has, over the years, dispensed and encouraged the dispensation of a large body of propaganda that I cannot help but believe has the calculated aim of eroding the will and virtues of the American people. Why this has been done is not so much a matter needing our discussion at this moment, but it is obvious that the effects of all this do not bode well for the liberties and freedoms of what we think of as our American republic.

"Now, I'm not saying that all wrongs, problems, and evils are the fault of the federal government. Of course that is not true. But if this government is 'of the people, by the people, and for the people,' then the people should own the government—not vice versa."

Robert replied, "I agree fully. Woodrow Wilson put it well when he said:

> The history of liberty is a history of limitations of governmental power, not the increase of it. When we resist, therefore, the concentration of power, we are resisting the powers of death, because concentration of power is what always precedes the destruction of human liberties.

"These truths," replied the doctor, "have been pushed out of the mainstream of national awareness along with this, from the Declaration of Independence: 'That whenever any form of government becomes destructive of these ends, it is the right of the people to alter or to abolish it . . .'

"'These ends' include truths that are, in the Declaration of Independence, called, 'self-evident,' and rights said to be 'certain unalienable Rights, that among these are life, liberty, and the pursuit of happiness.'

"It was when this right to life—guaranteed by our government—was taken away by the Supreme Court in 1973 and abortion on demand became the law that I realized the extent to which our people had been brainwashed and deceived. Women were promised liberation, and the carrot of freedom over their own bodies was dangled before them. But the Supreme Court placed women under a heavier bondage to men than ever. Instead of being free to choose, they are nearly always *expected* to face the loneliness, pain, and guilt of an abortion—or lose their boyfriends, acceptance of their parents, and sometimes even their husbands. Women have not been told how many of their unborn babies quiver for hours in the death throes of abandoned exposure. They don't stop to think for themselves, usually until it's too late, that this form of birth control makes them easier targets than ever for sexual exploitation by men.

"I deal with many women who have had abortions, and the truths surrounding these procedures have not been forthcoming from the media. Women themselves have generally been aborted from our culture—except as sex objects—yet they go along blindly accepting the propaganda of their 'status,' and the myths of their rights and freedoms, betraying themselves again and again by carrying their signs and parroting their slogans. The truth is, women's rights, like the rights of the general population, are being undermined by a constant media attack that cheapens human life. The sad thing is that one half of our population has had their most creative function maligned by a government that will prosecute the breaker of a bald eagle egg and smile at the killer of an unborn human.

"It was these things, Mr. Farr, that prompted me as a Christian to study some of the utterly destructive paths down which our country is being led."

Robert responded, "And I've also done some research and come to the same conclusions, but since my field is education, that's where I started. As you probably know, this country began to support its state religion of humanism with tax money in 1979 when the Department of Education came into full operation with a budget of forty billion dollars, ironically under the administration of a widely touted Christian president. Humanism, as I said the other day, is an illegal, government-sponsored religion that is a violent enemy of Christianity and traditional values. Another irony is the financial struggle of so many American parents to send their kids to colleges and universities only to have their values ridiculed and undermined by educators whose salaries are being paid by those very parents.

"As a teacher, I've seen organized pressure brought to bear on parents who object to the concept that the school system knows better than they what is best for their children. In fact, the going philosophy in many segments of the system is that the school, rather than the parents, own the children. This translates to state-owned children. I've seen parents shunned aside, ignored, and ridiculed behind their backs for objecting to books supporting witchcraft, incantations, and magic spells. These are religious in nature, although they're evil practices. Along with abortion, pornography, homosexuality, sexual promiscuity, and rebellion, these things come under the 'tolerant' umbrella of humanism. Tolerant, that is, of everything *except* Christianity.

"I have tried—unsuccessfully—to get books supporting witchcraft and magic spells removed from the *children's* section of the Wardensville Public Library! We are forced to have occult propaganda in our schools and libraries while we are prohibited from displaying any type of symbol relating to Christianity—even at Christmas.

"And what's more, there's increasing pressure to accept known homosexuals as teachers, and many of them are already in place. Think of the implications for our children who become victims of the behavior I was accused of in the meeting. And, AIDS—the first government-protected disease in history."

Dr. Johnson said, "I'm seeing more and more HIV positive women, and of course, their babies will be HIV positive—and the women's partners, and their other partners, if they have them . . .

"The point is," the doctor continued, "and the reason for our discussion is clear: the First Amendment to the Constitution of the United States is being flagrantly and illegally violated by the federal government. Congress and the Supreme Court have methodically instituted a man-centered religion and *mandated* its practice through the educational system. That this is beyond question is shown by the ruling of the Supreme Court in 1961 that humanism *is* a religion! You pointed this out in the meeting. Congress and the Supreme Court have methodically abridged the freedom of speech of Christians because, as you said, Christianity is completely foreign to humanism in any and all its various forms and practices such as abortions, homosexuality, pornography, occult practices, and certainly the philosophy known as New Age thought, which espouses almost anything anyone could think of—except Christianity. In short, humanism is humans worshipping themselves and doing as they please.

"Mr. Farr—" Dr. Johnson leaned forward in his chair, and he appeared to be searching Robert's face. The doctor's eyes asked the question even as his words made the statement: "We have one recourse left: 'the right of the people peaceably to assemble and to petition the government for a redress of grievances.'" Silence came again and ebbed. "They haven't taken that away—yet."

Robert felt his mouth become as hard as the man's eyes were soft. "Yet," he repeated with anger.

The other man's hand came to rest on his forearm. "You said—you wanted to."

Robert looked at that hand with its simple wedding band and wondered how it came to be here in this little room and place with women waiting and babies waiting and families waiting. To be delivered. The two stacks of golden hay on the wall captured in that fleeting moment of light unlike all other moments—sun coming through spaces in a wooden wall, a simple beam of gold on a little place in the hay. He could have done better. He had no hand like this doctor's, moved by knowledge hard-won through the centuries. But He could have. Just simple hay. Just simple men—and women. And children. "Yes. I want to."

"Good."

That night Robert sat in his accustomed place in the little church sanctuary pondering and knowing why it was called a sanctuary. Michael and Penny had gone dutifully to another room for children's prayer time while he and ten other adults sat in quietness before praying. She hadn't come to the cafeteria for lunch. He hadn't seen her all day, but he hadn't gone by the library. After he left Dr. Johnson's office he thought he should have but he hadn't called her even though, again, he thought he should have, and now he just sat there counting should haves and taking sanctuary in the stillness.

And Carol: only at the greatest distance possible had he seen her anymore, and then just her back. He should have called Beatrice. But maybe it was just as well; there could be no getting married until this mess was cleared up, and that wouldn't be anytime soon. And too, Dr. Johnson and some others had a plan, and now that plan included

Robert—to help "petition the government for a redress of grievances." Sanctuary—yes.

This being a time of meditation, Robert sat recalling another sanctuary and a time long gone like the oven. It was gas. At first his mother was afraid of gas, but then she wasn't. Probably . . . one of the best things about those days was the smell of clothes just ironed and her standing there shaking water out of an almost clear drink bottle with a red stopper top that had holes in it like a salt shaker when you looked at it up close. *You are the salt of the earth,* Jesus said, and Preacher Sutter had said that meant God uses Christians to keep society from rotting. Robert had repeated that one day when they had just come in from church after his mother asked him what the preacher said. When he told her, she had almost gotten excited, and after that Preacher Sutter was her favorite preacher of all times because he was so simple even a child could understand him. But Robert had not known what society was, and he thought you had to stay in jail in order to rot because that's what his mother always said about Uncle Jim, Dad's older brother. Uncle Jim drank, and Dad didn't like for him to stay in jail.

When she ironed, the clothes would smell good, even before they were ironed—like outdoors, like the wind on a day in March, and today is the first day in March. *March yourself right to bed, young man!* And once he did, all stiff with his chin pushed back into his throat and his arms snapping back and forth straight at his sides. She didn't like that at all, and neither did his dad.

But when she ironed, he would smell the clothes and think about outside and the fresh wind, or being cozy in his bed and warm. She wouldn't say anything, even about them being just folded. He wouldn't touch them except maybe sometimes with his nose, and if he had a cold, she would tell him to stay away. But then he couldn't smell them anyway. When she ironed sometimes she would look at him. And shake the bottle like . . . everything she was doing, all she had endured . . . everything she had ever learned—it was all there in her eyes, and it was all for him. It was as if in those times she would kind of nod to him with her eyes and give the bottle an extra hard shake like she wanted to emphasize something he didn't know yet. Like one day he might know, and *then* she would be proud of him.

One day he decided—he couldn't remember when—that he just didn't know if he liked it, or hated it when she ironed. Beatrice came to mind, standing in the doorway. Definitely he would call her. He should already have called.

Like a ride at a fair, one of those things with rides and shows that comes in October, his mind clanked forward to Paula's church. He had already known the lingo, and that impressed her right off the bat, his being able to talk church. He knew the words and when and how to use them, but God had used Paula to teach him the melody. She would sit beside him in her church, and they would hold hands. She had laughed and said that it wasn't a sin. She would just sit down beside him, like right now—

Now. Robert turned to his right and there she was, sitting there looking at him—Beatrice. He reached down and grabbed her hand tightly and sort of straightened his nose with his other hand as his face snapped forward so he could look to the front with his eyes closed as though something wonderful was about to happen there.

Robert still was not looking when Pastor John's voice welcomed all who had come. In his mind's eye he could see him standing there in his Wednesday night gray suit. Black hair, thirty-five years old. "We have had," the pastor was saying, "our time of preparation. All that has gone before has been to ready us for the moment at hand. God leaves nothing to chance."

Robert looked at the man in the gray suit and knew that Beatrice's hand must be hurting. Loosening his grip, he smiled, but not outwardly. Now he felt the strength of her hand, giving him back, he felt, his life.

"We should praise God for his providence," the pastor said.

I do, thought Robert as a rehearsal, *I do.*

"To that end, I shall read Psalm 107."

Their psalm, his and Paula's. As the words were read, he sat with eyes closed remembering them, and with each refrain his lips would move without sound:

Oh, that men would give thanks to the LORD for His goodness, and for His wonderful works to the children of men!

When the reading was over, there followed another silence, a great quiet that, for Robert, pressed his hand more tightly upon hers as he tried to meditate on the psalm but, falling before its words and the day, he could not. There in the sanctuary, he was remembering to die, and though he continued to sit upright, something inside pitched forward as into chest-high green grass and was gone beneath a mighty roar of silence. He had never seen him . . . he was always and only Grandpa Farr. Why think of him now? But the boy felt that he had known him.

The bottle with its salt shaker top. Sanctuary. Was also like— He should have called Beatrice. Thank God she had come.

The oven. It was gas.

And we never. Never, do you hear me? We—never— Bombed the railroad tracks. Never once. To Auschwitz. Never. And we knew—we knew.

He felt the tears on his face and her hand there, too. Grandpa was also a Christian, but—

Her hand, her fingers were soft and they helped . . . so much . . . thank God for her! *Oh, that men would give thanks to the LORD for His goodness, and for His wonderful works to the children of men!*

Carol, we wanted to see, we wanted to know, so now we know.

Now—we know.

I hope they . . .

The government knew. But they didn't do anything . . . about the tracks . . . to Auschwitz.

And Grandpa.

It had nothing to do with Paula," he said, "it had nothing to do with today, and yet it had everything to do with today." Then he told her all about the day and all the other days he thought might matter.

She cried, sitting there across from him in the booth at Benny's Grill as they drank root beer from iced-up mugs. He himself had no more need for tears, nor did he wonder why any more than a man wonders why as a child he was afraid of the dark because he still knows enough of that fear to understand. Her hand touched his with the coldness of ice in her fingertips like snowflakes at night when the world is silent under heavy white. Then summer clasped his hand and all the trees were green; her eyes shone clear and smiling.

"Do you realize," he said softly, "that this is the first time we've been together without children—or other people around? I mean—alone."

Beatrice grinned. "Yes."

They were leaning across the table gazing into each other's eyes, holding hands, and the jukebox was playing some old lullaby. "We're just like two kids sitting here like this," he thought aloud, almost smiling.

She nodded, and the look in her eyes caused him to glance downward to catch his breath. Fingers interlocking his were pressing, it seemed, swirling thoughts from his hands to somewhere behind his eyes, scattering—or threatening to scatter plans or whatever it was that he thought of as control. Shaking his head against the vertigo, he muttered, "I'm sorry."

"For what?" came her question and face in a simultaneity he was not ready for.

He shrugged and looked away. Carol stood in his memory: *Then stop telling me you're sorry!*

"What are you sorry for, Robert?"

He would be honest. "That I don't have a license."

"That you don't have a license to do what?"

"To marry you, Beatrice."

"Would you?"

"Yes, of course! We're engaged, remember?"

"I remember." She beheld the table and then their hands. "I remember—"

"What's wrong?"

"I don't want to always—just remember, Robert."

"What are you talking about?"

"Carol has strong feelings for you." Now she had his eyes, and he could not pull away.

"Yes—she does. It's called hate."

"No."

"You heard what she said."

"I heard what she said. And I saw how she ran away. And I saw how you looked. All of that came about because you told her about us."

"Beatrice—"

She paused. "Yes?"

"It's—she's married! The woman is married!"

"Yes, she's married. But that doesn't stop some people, and that doesn't stop some things—"

"Beatrice, I want you. I love you!"

"I know that. But nothing has ever stopped Carol Mayhew from getting what *she* wants."

"Did she say anything to you today?"

"No. She didn't come around."

"Beatrice, listen to me! I love you enough to marry you tomorrow, and we could go away. I mean we—"

"Robert—" She was shaking her head. "Listen to yourself! Do you really mean that? Could you—would you—*really* walk out on everything we've talked about tonight? Would you leave in the face of everything you've told me?"

He brought a hand to his forehead and passed it slowly downward over his eyes. "No."

She took that hand and reclaimed it on the table. "I love you too much to allow that. Neither of us would ever be happy or content if we ran away. Robert, you're confused. You're a typical man—in love."

"A typical man—" he echoed, half-thinking. "That's what she told me, too. But she didn't mention love."

"Why did she tell you that?"

"I had said something about not wanting to hurt her—I

mean, she had asked me not to—see—I mean, it was about her job. She asked me not to hurt her job."

Beatrice's eyes welled up, and she was staring down at their hands again and shaking her head back and forth.

"What's wrong?"

"Nothing," she replied with a breaking voice.

"Please, tell me. Please, Beatrice—"

She raised her head, and her tears released. "Some women—" She swallowed hard and went on. "—love a man . . . who's honest . . . and . . . simple."

He was looking at the top of her head as she pressed a napkin to her eyes. "Beatrice—"

She shook her head for him to be quiet.

"I don't love her."

Her head shook again. "Shh," she replied as if listening for something he could not know.

Robert leaned against the back of the booth, still holding one of her hands. He wondered mightily what it was that she was crying about.

They sat like this for a minute or so, and an old man and woman shuffled over to the door where the old man helped the woman on with her coat in a ritual that appeared as practiced as it was slow. They seemed not to have noticed Robert and Beatrice, but just before pulling the wooden door shut behind him, the man looked at them for more than a heartbeat. His mouth pressed into all the knowing he could have and then he was gone, the old door standing closed in a silence that denied they had ever been there.

Without effort, doorways came marching from the nooks and corners of somewhere to line up as one door might when seen in two mirrors facing each other. She stood in all of them in the night with a white box in her hands while from all the doors something was fleeing away like a dazed and frightened bird blown by a mighty wind through a window left open by a child who had forgotten what she had done down dusky halls, crying out in fear of the dark.

In her hands she had brought life and in her eyes, and she would never want him dead—nor did the other—even in their losing. From the outside, even he knew, his stone house looked so simple. Yet, when snow makes pink the sky in its coldness, there are so many inside. But only one—for him—because she had come through that door.

Simple. Robert smiled to himself in sadness that she did not know how simple it all was and why it was that she cried at winning as though it were defeat. Or fear of the dark outside. Where she would never be again.

He would give her a ring. Perhaps then she would know. Or begin to believe him.

"Beatrice, look at me, please." She did, through streaming eyes. "I have chosen you. I would die . . . to have you in my life."

She nodded and went back to the napkin.

"Listen to me," he all but whispered, "dry your eyes. You're too beautiful to cry." Now her shoulders shook, and she made a little moaning sound. Robert slipped around the end of the booth and sat beside her, taking her in his arms. She was clinging to him tightly and crying softly into his sweater. "Shh," he whispered several times as he rocked her gently back and forth.

Finally she was leaning on him and looking up from

under his arm. She tried to raise up, but he held her fast. "Robert—" she said into his muffling sweater.

"Benny doesn't care," he offered. "In fact, he's in the back, and no one else is here."

"My neck hurts."

"Oh—okay . . . So I'm a pain in the neck."

"Let me sit up straight, please."

He turned her loose, and she set about making repairs with the comb and compact she took from her purse. "I look a fright," she murmured.

"You sure do! I was so scared, I didn't know what to do."

She gave him a quick glance and replied, "You sure couldn't prove it by me!"

"Oh—"

She laughed, blew her nose, and put the compact away.

Robert slid closer, and she said, "It's probably bedtime for the Swensons, don't you think?"

"Who're the Swensons?"

"They're the couple from church who are keeping Michael and Penny, and if it's not their bedtime, it's certainly the children's."

"Why are you so interested in bed?"

She turned her head as if to look away, but her eyes never left his. "It's natural for us to want what's right for children." She smiled, and he kissed her as she did, tenderly then harder until she pushed away. "Robert—"

He put a finger over her lips. "I want very much for us to do what's natural . . . for a child."

"I know, but . . ."

"Beatrice, I want you to have our baby. I want a child by you."

"I do, too—so much more than you could ever know! To have your life inside me."

"Our life."

"Yes, our life. Robert, I love you so much!" She turned away as if she were going to cry again but instead raised her head to stare at where the far wall and the ceiling came together.

"What are you thinking?" he asked.

She did not answer immediately, but at length looked at him and said, "About having a baby. I had thought there would never be one for me, and I . . . well—"

"Go on."

"I thought you might not want one."

"Well, I do."

"It's strange, Robert—how we can sometimes want something so much that we just assume it can never be."

"I know."

"And sometimes we make a religion out of not having it."

Now he looked at the wall . . . at all the walls lining up and closing in and making halls. And at the one outside the law office he had called reality. "Tell me," he said, closing his eyes, "why did you use the puzzle that day?"

"Why?"

Her repetition of the question was like a boy shooting an arrow far out over a field all brown in the breath-steaming coldness of winter. The arrow in flight recalls everything the boy has ever known, and he feels this without giving it much thought because he's a boy and can do those things and can even call the arrow a star in the blue sky as it flies toward forever, not certain to ever come to earth or be found again. But the arrow is not a star, and that moment did not hold all he knew, and he had found the arrow . . . not far away at all, he realized now as he opened his eyes.

"So they might learn that something simple can be beyond their understanding and abilities."

For some time Robert didn't say anything, then he murmured, "That goes against the current philosophy: 'Dream it—do it.'"

"And we both know that philosophy is dead wrong."

"Yes."

"Robert," she said, facing him and leaning against the wall with her stockinged feet up on the seat and her knees almost under her chin, "when do you want to get married?"

"When we get this mess behind us."

"Why?"

"My future is uncertain. I may not have a job soon."

"Why do you say *your* future instead of *our* future?"

"I guess I've lived solo for so long that it's just habit."

"Is it? Is it a habit—or a religion?"

"I've never thought of it that way, but I suppose . . ." He trailed the sentence off.

"I'm not going to push you, Robert—ever. But there are a couple of things you need to know."

"Such as?"

"If you lose your job, it's not the end of the world."

"Beatrice, I'm not going to ask you to get into a situation with an unemployed schoolteacher with two kids and no chance to get any kind of job in this town with all the furor this mess is liable to raise, and no money to move somewhere—"

"Robert, please—listen to me."

"Okay."

"I have money."

"No! I'm not about to—"

"You said you would listen."

"All right, I'll listen."

"My father was a farmer, but he also invested. He did well—very well—then got out of the market. Between his investments and an inheritance, there's about half a million dollars rolling over every year in cash deposits. He's already given everything to me. There's the money plus the farm, plus three hundred acres of prime hardwood timber."

Robert made no reply, but turned and faced the back of the other seat.

"It's all ours, Robert."

"No," he said breathily. "It belonged to your father. Now, it's yours."

"It would belong to us. And besides—you may not lose your job."

"No. You and your family worked for what you have. I contributed nothing. There's no way I would come in and—"

"Then you don't love me."

"Come on, Beatrice—you know better than that!"

"Do I? If I had nothing, that would be all right, wouldn't it?"

"It would be different."

"Of course. It would be more like what you're used to. Robert, what gives you the right to dictate the terms of what God wants?"

"I'm not dictating anything."

"Yes you are. You know what I think? I think you're afraid to get married! You say: 'when this mess is over.' Then you say, in effect, 'You have too much money for me to marry you.' One excuse is as good as another when you're scared."

He turned to her face above her knees. "Do you think I'm scared?"

"I know you are."

He beheld her without saying anything and then turned toward the other seat.

"Aren't you?"

He opened his mouth, paused, and then said, "Yes."

Beatrice laughed. "So am I."

"What are we so afraid of?"

"Only God knows, Robert."

In a few moments, he said, "You know what?"

"What?"

"It's past the kids' bedtime."

She slipped her feet into her shoes on the floor, kissed him on the cheek, and made as though to push him out of the booth. They stood, and he went to the counter and placed a five dollar bill under a salt shaker. "Good night, Benny," he called to the diamond-shaped window in the kitchen door.

An old man's voice replied, "Good night, Robert."

He took her hand and walked her to the outside door

which he opened for her. As they were going out, he paused and looked back at the booth where they had sat, at the empty mugs on the table. They went out, and he closed that ancient door quietly behind them.

Robert awoke Friday morning from what seemed an endless line of doors curving through walls that moved about like certain carnival rides—fixed to predetermined paths but baffling to the riders. As the dream vanished, he felt a desperate need to know where he was, that he could not go on without knowing. But with the dying of the alarm under his hand and the return of normal breathing, the desperation diffused into something like logical thought so quickly that he hardly did more than reckon that he must have been dreaming something.

The why-I-shouldn't pounding gave way to the serene ceiling of the day he felt approaching in the window's outline. Situations would not float off into the blue infinity. *There are limits,* he told himself; *there is a beginning, and there will be an end.* There are boxes called rooms to contain fragrances such as he knew now . . . hers and her softness that he had breathed in as she leaned on him in the booth two nights ago. And last night's when she didn't push away in the darkness outside her apartment door and how he had known she couldn't push away anymore. But she had whispered a word—an ancient and forgotten word that he knew was right. Beatrice had said, "No," and with that delicate sound in his ear, he had left, and now he was very glad. Without setting out to do so, Robert realized as he pondered the ceiling, they had shown each other a faithfulness that would be vital to their marriage. As Paula had said, sex before marriage is sex outside marriage, and sex outside marriage kills the meaning of marriage. So Paula had insisted on a real marriage, and Robert knew now that he and Beatrice were also going to have one.

But—when? he wondered as he got out of bed. *When?* To be real—it needed to be soon. But the situation of his pride, as she called it—what about that? What about the room called today and all the things and situations that would come into it, and all the situations and things brought forward from all the other rooms and days and times—like columns of addition problems, being carried over, adding up, and always changing?

They would be moving. After the wedding. Most likely to the farmhouse for just a short while. A time for settling in and adjusting without the hassle of selecting another house or having one built or making major decisions of the kind involving neighborhoods, schools, and the like. Her parents would be no problem—they would simply move, too. To their brick house on Firetower Road on the edge of the three hundred acres of prime hardwood timberland. They stayed there part of the time, anyhow, because there was a pond, and they liked to fish. What did they think about Robert—even though they had not met him, and all they knew about him was what she had told them? They trusted her judgment and looked forward to getting to know him. *Really? Yes, really.* She said he would probably come to love them as much as she did, and that no one ever had better parents.

Robert lathered up into a reminder of a white-bandaged buddy with his face blown away lying on a hospital bed in Norfolk, Virginia. He started shaving, recalling what Billy-boy had said all through basic training, that he knew all the ins and outs. All the ins and outs . . . *No outs, it's the bottom of the third with a runner on first. Switch-hitting Mick is at bat. He's hitting left-handed today . . . and it's a beau-ti-ful day here at Yankee Stadium. The flag in centerfield is barely moving. Here's the windup . . . the pitch—Mantle swings . . .* You could hear the wooden bat meeting that ball head-on over the radio. You could see the dirt in the batter's box lined with white lime as the Mick towered over the world in that twisted-wrist follow-through that said this ball is history. It rose as high as the wild cheering that sounded like putting your ear to half a bottle of soft drink after you've shaken it with your thumb over the mouth. It cleared the centerfield fence, and the flag waved good-bye as the ball passed over it on its way to becoming a white star in a boy's blue memory box that he hadn't even seen.

Wonder if Daniel had ever seen the Mick play? Wonder if he had storebought memories or if his were homemade by a radio because a TV was too expensive? Robert wondered as he had wondered what Billy-boy Doaks would have said if he had had a mouth under the white plaster. And a jaw. But he didn't wonder long, because Billy-boy got a pencil and paper and scrawled, *Semper Fi*. Always faithful. But the whole country hadn't cared about Billy-boy, or Daniel—

Or Grandpa.

They cared more about a ball game than a war. And they sang the anthem of the beer that had gotten Paula outta here. And put her in his memory box. And now they wanted him to say *Semper Fi* and go along as they marched—goose-stepping on their blood. And the blood of the One who died on a cross but wasn't dead anymore. Anymore—Robert Farr wasn't going to say his *Semper Fi* to them. He wiped the traces of lather from his face and looked long in the mirror. "*Semper Fi*," he said to the unseen God who wasn't dead anymore. "Amen."

When he arrived at school he went straight to the principal's office, not feeling like a visitor anymore but knowing exactly what to do. Exactly. At least for the next two days—and after that he would do what he had to do, thinking all the while and knowing what he had learned while shaving, that it's amazing how clear and ordered situations and things become once a major decision has been made. For example: marriage. That was unusual, he knew, for things to line up so clearly behind one decision, but that situation had been put into his life as a kind of signpost, a clear indication that there is a purpose, a plan, and that nothing is left to chance. When the correct decision is made for the right reason, he was sure now, things work out. But it requires faith, and faith results in action, and action there was going to be. Robert marveled that while he had known the words all along, he had just encountered the melody again after so much discord and static. And it had all become clear while shaving, while looking for the child in the mirror.

Carol was not in, so he stood at her window looking out at the morning sky and its way of changing. Clouds rolled up like steel bars slanting over the horizon were slowly giving way to the sun somewhere out there or behind there or down there, depending on one's perspective. But it was the same sun and the same clouds regardless. The Master was at the organ men called the universe, and the great swell stop was full out. Every note, every jot has a purpose. Even in a rest there is music, and the refrain was bearing him up like a wave to the blue sky above the clouds as seas thundered and mountains rang with the descant of purpose.

"What do *you* want?" asked Carol's voice behind him.

He turned to face her, but now things were different. "I want to tell you something—something you need to know."

"What do I need to know—from you?"

"The evolution seminar tomorrow at State—I've decided to go! I'm going to that seminar, Carol. And I'm going to stand up and confront the presenter at every point of error!"

The woman grabbed her head and turned quickly away to totter momentarily like an old-fashioned spinning top as it runs down. "No, no, no, no." She was shaking her head and releasing the words over and over as though life itself were escaping through her lips. "I'm not believing this! I'm not believing this! This is *not* happening . . . it's *not*!"

"Denial has always been your favorite tactic, Carol."

She stopped, frozen, it seemed, with her hands to her head. "Why are you doing this?"

"You wanted me to go, remember? You said I was *afraid* to go."

"Okay! I retract that! I'm sorry I said it; I apologize!"

"That's all too late. I don't want your apology. I don't want anything from you."

She spun to confront him. "What do you want? Money? Look—I'll pay you not to go! How much do you want?"

"You're out of control, Carol—and it's not very becoming. Just stop and collect yourself."

"Shut up! You just shut up!" The woman walked in what struck him as a morbid high-heeled prance to her desk, but once there, she turned around, went back to the door, and closed it. She returned to the desk and stood there begging with her eyes before saying, "Please, Robert, don't go. Teachers, faculty, principals, superintendents—from all over this part of the state—" her voice softened, "—are going to be there. Please, I beg you, don't go."

"Carol, you once told me that it wouldn't matter if they pulled your certification." Robert hastened to interrupt her reply with, "Besides—we can work it so it will look very good for you! Just stand up, yourself, and denounce me as an ignorant, simpleminded bumpkin! Tell them I'm crazy! Wash your hands of me before them all. Tell them that I'm even now in the process of being removed from the system. Carol, tell them anything you want—*anything*—and I give you my word that I won't reply to a single charge you bring against me—not one!

"This is your chance, Carol, to be rid of me and my simplemindedness forever! Every one of those people—those people you're so afraid of—every one of them will be on your side! You'll get your wish, Carol! You'll actually get to see it!"

Her eyes had been welling up; now two smudges of mascara etched downward, but she wiped them away with her fingers. Then a sob burst forth into her hands, and with a sudden lurch of shoulders, she was sitting at her desk wailing out grief and pain that she violently hated with her bowed and shaking head. Robert started toward her in what he took to be understanding but stopped. He knew, but he could not understand. Puzzled, he watched as he had with Beatrice, and wondered mightily what it was that she was crying about. "Carol, I . . ."

She just shook her head harder and cried all the louder. Robert thought about leaving, about going to the door, waiting for a lull and slipping out . . . hearing the silence of the door as it didn't make any sound closing behind him. He thought of himself walking down the hall, still wondering, and going into his room remembering the grief descanting her voice, and it was that—that part of her that he knew—and something he shared with her but could not understand that kept him there waiting. What could it be that so completely tore her soul?

He heard people walking in the outer office and knew they were looking through the door's glass to see it all. But what did they see? He didn't know.

At length she sat at her desk with her face in her hands. The scene grew more intense as the sound of walking became the sound of tiptoeing. Then the sound of standing—complete silence. His back—perhaps—hid her from them, and he wished that it could be so, but it could not: the narrow wall to the right of the door was glass. So Carol would know too of the peering and whispering. He wanted so much to go to her and pick her up in his arms, as he had Beatrice from the floor, and find her laughing. And tell her that whether its laughing or crying, a boy or a girl, it all depends on the melody that she could only hear with her heart. That it's our duty on hearing it to rise up until we see the velvet jungle below us and to be alive now—by faith—as we go back in.

So in his mind and heart he did that while he stood there unmoving. He lifted her up and carried her gently out the window behind her—out past the circle where once it had rained and where Charlie had dug in and the choppers moved out. Out where they couldn't see her or hurt her anymore. Out to where a sunbeam was slanting down through bars of steel and clouds, and in his arms he carried her up that sunbeam and presented her to his Brother who had died in the war and who wasn't dead anymore. And He smiled because He had enabled Carol to hear His melody in her heart. Then, He, Himself, wiped away her tears, and there were no more of them.

Carol stood up behind her desk with a remarkably composed face. "Robert—" was all she said while her eyes moved about to meet, he felt sure, those of any individual who might dare to even glance in now. Then her gaze came to rest on him for a time longer than he could understand before she spoke. "I can't do any of those things. I shan't insult your—" she paused and seemed to be struggling to continue, "—your faith. I won't insult that by telling you why I can't carry out your suggestions."

"I don't understand. You hate my faith. According to you, Christianity is the cause of most of the world's problems. You've called us a bunch of 'right-wing religious zealots.' Now you say you don't want to insult my faith. Carol, has anyone ever told you that you're a little strange? Or does that come naturally from always getting everything you ever wanted?"

"Haven't you?"

"Haven't I what?"

"Always gotten everything you ever wanted?"

"You've got to be kidding! My dad couldn't even afford a car until—"

"I'm not talking about things, Robert. Things don't run your life."

"What are you talking about?"

She shrugged, smiled, and seemed to change somehow. "Nothing. We all have to do what we have to do. Go to the seminar, and do what you have to do."

"All I'm going to do is point out the truth."

"And what is truth?"

He took half a step toward her. "What you just called 'nothing.'"

"You're good with words. And I say you have always gotten what you wanted."

"No. No, I haven't."

"What was the big thing in life that you didn't get, Robert?"

His hand fumbled with the compass in his pocket. "I didn't get to keep my wife, and I didn't get to have my parents stay together."

"Does your parents' divorce still bother you?"

"Sometimes."

"Why?"

He glanced away, then fastened his gaze back on her. "That's something—I don't know."

After a few moments, she said, "Well, I guess we have nothing else to talk about."

"I don't know that either."

"Oh? Well, when is the wedding?"

"We haven't set a date."

"Well, I would have thought that if you're sure—"

"My future's so uncertain—I find it hard to involve someone else."

"You're still afraid, Robert."

"Maybe—"

"Maybe—we *do* have some other things to talk about."

"Perhaps. But it would deal with what you call 'nothing.'"

Her face softened. "But—of course." She turned at a little angle to him, crossed her arms, and asked, "How far do you intend to go with your protest?"

"All the way. I've composed some letters. I'm going to do everything I can to cause at least a few people to see that the government—with the full cooperation of the media—has relentlessly undermined people's faith in the Bible and has illegally instituted a man-centered state religion."

Her only reply was to curl her bottom lip up between her teeth.

"Let me ask you this," Robert continued. "Do you honestly think I'm crazy? Do you think—"

"I think," she interrupted, "that people don't want to hear the truth. They don't care anymore."

"But do you think I'm right?"

"Does it make a difference what I think?"

"Yes."

"Why?"

"I respect you."

She glanced disappointedly at the floor and faced him again. "I don't buy into your belief in the Bible, Robert. But, I've thought a lot about this, and I've talked with Cyrus. I believe what you say about the government, the media, and the state religion is all true."

He drew a sharp breath. "Carol! You do? I mean . . ."

"You're right, Robert. Cyrus says there's no question about the state religion and its illegality. He has some reservations about the part played by the media."

"This is amazing! I thought—"

"That I couldn't be objective? You're wrong there. I can be very objective. I know how to evaluate . . . evidence."

"Carol, listen!" he ordered, taking another step toward her. "Do you see how the whole thing—humanism in its entirety—is based squarely on evolution?"

"Of course. I know there are major problems with evolution, but I still believe it's basically true. I also see why the myths of Genesis have to be dispelled. Christianity has to have the creation account and what you call original sin.

Any form of evolution would have humans developing so slowly that when you got to the first creature we could call human, he or she would have been determined by natural selection to do what you call sin—as with any other tendency—so that there would be no real choice, or certainly no real responsibility, because sin would have had to be evolving along with everything else. Randomness would have been in effect—not choice."

Robert was waving his arms up and down and laughing in joy. Carol gave him a concerned look and almost stepped backward as he came gesticulating forward saying, "Great! Great! Good—Carol, that's good! That's right! You got it! You got it!"

Standing her ground, she stopped him, saying, "You're out of control, Robert! And it's not very becoming."

Still smiling, he replied, "Yes it is! It's very becoming—"

"For you, maybe."

"Yes! For me! For me, it's a way of life!" He stood smiling down at her and drinking in her uncertain eyes as they dropped under lids heavy with lashes.

"Don't think," she said to his left elbow bent somewhere at his side, "that I'm any kind of believer. I've read some—and thought. And I'm objective. I have an open mind, that's all."

"But," Robert said, allowing a long pause to follow, a time sufficient to cause her to require his thought with her full face. "Why? Why," he said, "were you pleading for me not to go to the seminar a few minutes ago? Why, suddenly, do you tell me to go and do what I have to do? I don't understand."

Her face dropped seemingly to confront a button on his coat momentarily, then she followed her eyes around to the window behind her as if she had heard someone call her name. Carol stood looking, perhaps at the blue where the steel clouds had been, or at the circle where everything had once been in its nothing-newness under the sun: where choppers were moving out overhead and men's blood ran dripping bright red on green ribbons of life called grass . . . where a corpsman was like an angel . . . and boys swathed in bloody bandages died calling Mama.

She stood for some time beholding the place where it all was, yet without seeing, for she could not know. But then she said his name, and he wondered and then knew from the sound she made that she had her own war and her jungle of whatever color, as she had once said without meaning to. "It's you I worry about," she said quietly. "Not me."

Then she turned around and looked at him strongly. "I've said enough. Now, go and do what you have to do."

Robert did not move.

"Don't say anything—just go."

She didn't speak again, but just looked at him until he started to turn away. He paused at her door to look at her. Carol's back was turned; she was facing the window.

CHAPTER

12

That day had gone, leaving traces of itself standing about in his mind like certain yellow spring flowers blasted by a sudden nighttime frost. Always, over and through all the things that had come into that day, he would remember her standing there by the window as he was leaving. Yet, it was his going that began the day and ended it too, it seemed, with her standing.

Stacy Robertson was the next to speak to him, down in his room waiting. He should know, she said, about this: a certain letter going out to the parents and guardians of certain students, all students he had taught here at Jefferson. And two other classes—selected at random—so no one could say for sure what was happening. There was an effort, said the letter, to enhance the total effectiveness of Jefferson Elementary's program, so these enquiries were being sent to parents and guardians—selected at random—to see if there were any comments, not previously noted, concerning the treatment of children at the school. There were other questions about lunches, buses, and skills in the letter that seemed to be more its subject.

Stacy thought he should know, she said, because Mayhew-Barr had typed the letter herself and asked her confidential help one day at lunch when the two secretaries were gone. Stacy had selected the other two classes and had been asked to check again to see that none of Mr. Farr's students, past or present, had been left out. What could the woman be up to, now? she wondered.

It was then that Carol took her place—standing by the window as he was leaving—indelibly in his mind. *Don't worry about this,* he had said to Stacy. *This is good. Very good.*

So Stacy had gone from the room and the day leaving him holding a copy of the letter. And the woman standing.

The next day was Saturday, and it came seeping around the blinded window's outline into his awareness before the alarm. Other Saturdays lined up behind this one all the way back to that fishing trip with the sun on his father's face as he baited the hook. And all the way up to the farm with Beatrice and the children a week ago.

There was no way he could know the contents of this day, it seemed his mind kept saying to itself as he showered, shaved, and had a breakfast of oatmeal, toast, and coffee. There was another phrase, "little note, nor long remember," from Lincoln's remarks at Gettysburg, that seemed to rise up behind him like an ancient stand of timber out of which he had just come as through a door opening onto a sprawling field shrouded in fog, swirling smoke and now silent cannon, and occasional flashes as of lightning. It was his, this day to thus advance over uncertain ground that could not even be seen. And though he did not consider it for very long, there was a feeling that somewhere out there he might again encounter a solitary tree emerging from the fog and that it would bid him onward with cold and barren outstretched arms.

After an hour's drive he arrived at the parking lot across the street from Kaiser Hall on the campus of State University. For a few minutes he sat in the car watching groups and broken lines of people walking toward the main entrance of the building from various places on two parking lots. Beatrice would be having breakfast with Michael and Penny now at the only home table the kids had ever known. Then they would go to the farm and ride if it didn't rain; rain was forecast, but it hadn't rained yet, although the sky was think and cloudy. She hadn't had much to say, but she had held him and kissed him and said that she would be praying.

They had talked at some length about this. And Robert had talked—well, actually consulted—with Dr. Allen Johnson. Robert would almost certainly be arrested and charged with disorderly conduct, although he had no intention of being anything like disorderly. Since the focus of the seminar was upon "countering attacks upon evolution by the uninformed," he was simply going to request that he be allowed to rebut throughout the presentation for a realistic demonstration of the focus. He would ask for no more than two minutes per rebuttal and would stand at every point where he could cite scientific evidence against what the presenter was saying. What Robert modestly hoped would be an honest debate, Dr. Johnson had predicted would end with his arrest.

He got out of the car and, carrying his brown attaché case, joined those walking toward the building. It seemed natural to want to tell himself that this was not for his life, that these men and women going along behind him and in front of him were all like himself. They were laughing—a few of them—and some talked quietly. They carried briefcases—some of them—and a sweater or two, and there were some umbrellas. His index finger straightened to lay momentarily flat along the handle of the case as if it might have been the trigger housing of the M-16 with the safety off and the weapon set for automatic fire. *Charlie's in the area*—he didn't think that but felt it in the fist tightening again in his gut. *Recon said so. The next thing you see move or hear on either side of this line, you are going to kill. Jungle on both sides and the guy in front and the guy behind are the best friends in the world—family—and I don't even know their names, and it's gonna happen any second . . . it's gonna break loose . . . it's gonna happen . . . any second—* And it breaks loose—The rifle's kicking, and the jungle's flying all to green pieces everywhere you pull that thing across. Staccato thunder deafens, echoes, and deafens. Then the firing is sporadic, dropping to silence, and there were a couple of grenades you remember going off. You watch and listen and hear moaning up the path. But there's some from out there in the jungle, too. There's some shooting at those sounds. Somebody throws another grenade, and after that the only moaning is up the line. They were nearly to the door, and he didn't feel any kinship or family with anybody in this line. More like Charlie's in the area.

Inside the building, Robert followed the clacking steps of the people in front of him down a wide hall gleaming under electrified fluorescence and buffed wax. A laser-printed sign on a wooden stand marked the registration area, a line of tables where several university students wearing name tags sat thumbing through stacks of cards, writing on sheets of paper, and talking to registrants. He went to the table marked with a sign reading 'Unregistered,' signed in, and got a manila envelope bulging with material, including a name tag, which he filled out and attached to his coat. He asked the student if Dr. Melvin Scott, the presenter, happened to be in the area, and she described the man but said she didn't see him just then.

Robert walked through open double doors and a few meters into the huge, semicircular auditorium that sloped steeply down to a low stage with a table and a podium in the center. Books and magazines lay on the table, and probably a couple of hundred people sat scattered around the lecture hall. Their indistinct low murmuring and variously colored clothing would have instilled the usual grin-and-bear-it attitude Robert normally adopted at these infrequent times when a Saturday was taken out of the week—but not today. The knot in his gut was tighter and actually hurting; his palms felt clammy, and he didn't see how he could do this at all.

The bed had been his staging area last night, not a sleeping place. He had prepared as he rolled and turned and sweated. Robert Farr had already been this afraid . . . last night. More afraid than he had ever been in Vietnam, and there are different kinds of fear and maybe different kinds of death. He had family then, guys he knew and when they were gone, guys he didn't know, but they were still family. *Semper Fi* guys who watched each other's back, and he just didn't see how this was going to work. There's no way this thing can work, no way that he could see.

He put the case down and looked at his hands. Robert had never done this in Nam. They were steady, not shaking in the least. It was strange and a little surprising to think what he was thinking, to think the thought that just came into his head like the wind had blown it in, tousling his hair like the day at the wall—the one in D.C. when he had traced their names with his fingers and cried, and the one at the law office when he had faced reality. It was really strange to think that you have seen your hands before. And feel something like that once—a long time ago—they were big and scary. His hands—his father's hands were baiting the hook. And Robert remembered the sun had been on his father's face. And he had smiled.

Robert looked straight out over the stage and the podium. There was a blue curtain up there across the front, and he looked there at the curtain and held the compass tightly in his hand deep in his pocket. In a few moments, he bowed his head and almost silently whispered, "Amen."

He picked up the case and laid his index finger momentarily along the handle. Turning, he saw a man fitting the presenter's description standing in the doorway. The man started toward him, and Robert moved out into the center of the aisle, changing the case to his left hand as he did. The man's name tag identified him as Dr. Mel Scott, and Robert extended his hand. "Sir, I'm Robert Farr. It's a pleasure to meet you."

"Hello, Robert," said the professor from under black eyebrows speckled with gray as he shook hands. He had a ready smile and little hair, and the corners of his eyes seemed wrinkled with humor as well as with age. "I'm glad to meet you."

"Sir," said Robert, releasing his hand, "I should tell you that I'm an informed disbeliever in evolution. Since this seminar focuses upon confronting opponents of the theory, I'm asking for the privilege of responding several times, for no more than two minutes each time, to some of your remarks."

The man took a step back and eyed Robert up and down with his face slacked in discernible surprise. Yet when he spoke, he seemed an old hand at such confrontations. "This is not a debate, and I'm not going to be interrupted during the presentation! There will be two occasions for questions, and I'll take one from you each time. That's all!"

The professor started toward the platform, but Robert said, "No, sir, that's not all! This seminar focuses upon confronting opponents of evolution, and I'm an opponent. I'm not going to allow you to build your usual straw man and knock it over for these people!"

The man's face hardened in flushed anger. "You interrupt once, and I'll have you removed from this auditorium!"

"Then, respectfully, sir, I suggest that you make provisions for that before you begin. I also suggest that you have security people called to carry out your wishes and police on hand to arrest me, because I'm not going to be lightly brushed off!"

The professor again looked Robert up and down, then turned and stormed back up the aisle and out the door while those on the back row stared at him and then at Robert. Turning around, Robert saw numerous faces looking at him from over the backs of seats. Across the auditorium a woman in a red coat stood up. It was Carol Mayhew-Barr, and she just stood there looking at him with her hands at her sides. Their eyes were locked for those moments across the auditorium slowly filling with audible speculations and questions that he hardly heard, and a few people were still coming in. Then a movement at the double doors turned his head, and he saw two uniformed men and Dr. Scott pointing at him. He nodded deeply to them, and the doctor walked down the aisle and past him while the security men remained in the hall. Robert followed a few meters behind the professor and stopped at the second row of seats. As he turned to sit down in the aisle seat, he saw Carol also sitting down.

Dr. Scott was behind the podium, not saying anything for what seemed a long time. He looked around, probably at everyone there, adjusted the microphone on the podium, and said, "Good morning. I'm Melvin Scott, head of the Department of Humanities at Pan Commonwealth University, Lebanon, Kansas. We are here today to gain a better understanding of what we are about as educators and why we must more sharply define our goals of liberating the 'huddled masses yearning to breathe free.' For those of you who might not know, that phrase is from the poem of Emma Lazarus at the Statue of Liberty.

"Liberty has many facets, but liberty has no meaning if the mind is not free, and it is the unique task of education to free the mind. The shackles of ignorance, fear, superstition—and that especially includes religion—must be thrown off. It is our task as educators to remove all restraints from human potential—all restraints. What began as a random flicker of life in primeval cosmology must continue to evolve upward to absolute perfection. Humans stand well within the threshold of mastery of the forces that have shaped us, so that *we*—our generation—are truly the New Age. We are beginning to choose and determine, that is, to engineer, our own evolution and thus our destiny. The causes and effects of the process were once ignorantly assigned to the whims of the gods, but these causes and effects are now our territory! We educators are the high priests of the true religion! Knowledge and understanding results in power—power to rise up and be our own gods, to throw away the shackles of any and all outside authority!"

The professor paused and looked around as if he expected a word of agreement, but there was only silence. Now his eyes blazed, and he raised a fist to emphasize each word. "Evolution is the absolute bedrock, the absolute foundation of our educational system!" He dropped his fist as a hand to the podium and continued. "To deny evolution is to return to the dark ages! To deny evolution is to say that there are things we cannot ever know, and this is blasphemy! Give humans enough time, and we'll know everything that is. Give us enough time, and there is no problem we cannot solve. To set any kind of limit on our ability to know blasphemously denies our calling and our identity—and the identity of our students and our students' students. Given enough time—"

Robert stood. "WHO ARE YOU ASKING TO GIVE US THIS TIME? WHERE DOES TIME COME FROM?"

The professor's eyes burnt into his for several moments of hot silence. Then he looked around the auditorium and said, "This is a classic example of the kind of addiction to ignorance that we must confront and overcome."

"WHY?" Robert cried, "IS ASKING A QUESTION AN ADDICTION TO IGNORANCE?"

"Good question!" shouted a man in the audience.

The man at the podium slowly smiled and leaned closer to the microphone. With a softer voice he said, "This exchange points to the need for this seminar." He straightened up and said, looking at Robert, who was still standing, "Fear often asks such questions."

Robert responded, "YES—THE FEAR OF FALSEHOOD!"

"What *is* falsehood?" asked the professor, and he walked over to the table and picked up one book or magazine after another and dropped each in turn. Back at the microphone, he said, "The mind determines what is false. What I read and experience must square with my mind, with my educated powers of ascertaining reality. You see, Mr. Farr," he paused, glanced at the ceiling, and with strong emphasis said, "the only limits are those of our minds, and only education can remove those limits! Evolution and education are essentially the same in that both eliminate mistakes and falsehood."

Robert started toward the platform, and the professor warned, "Mr. Farr, I've already taken enough time with you, and the guards are standing by to remove you!" Lifting a hand and leaning forward toward the microphone with an air of confidentiality, he said, "Here comes a man who has already indicated his intention of being arrested! I'm going to cooperate by briefly allowing this individual to help us carry out our purpose of confronting the uninformed." To Robert, who was now standing beside him, he said, "I'm going to give you two minutes of time. After that, if you do not return to your seat and stay there—in silence—I want the guards to come and remove you!" The man stepped back and glanced at his watch.

"Thank you for this personal privilege," Robert said. "Everything you have said—every word—is based on a fallacy that has been disproved billions upon billions of times, and never once has this fallacy been shown to be true. Everything that Dr. Scott has said requires a known, easily verifiable law of physics to be completely false! The second *law* of thermodynamics is just that—a law, verifiable at will. The *theory* of evolution is nothing more than a complete denial of reality as we know it. The second *law* of thermodynamics insists that while energy everywhere in the universe cannot be diminished, the energy available for work—or progress, as opposed to decay—is constantly becoming less. In other words, water flows downhill and has energy to carry matter with it. But when it reaches the bottom of the hill, its potential is still there, but it has no energy to get back up the hill. The second *law* of thermodynamics states that matter always behaves this way! This *law* says that order comes first, and disorder always follows! For example, see if your automobile is improved if you leave it neglected outdoors for twenty years! Yet, evolutionists would have us believe that nonliving atoms were randomly arranged—that is, by chance—into ordered organisms that moved back uphill by themselves, eventually to think for themselves, and finally to be their own gods! Science depends on observation, yet not once has science observed a natural exception to the second law of thermodynamics!

"Can anyone," Robert said loudly, "in this auditorium—or in the world—deny what I have said?" His pause was a silence broken only by a solitary cough. "Now," continued Robert after another moment, "it has taken one minute to *scientifically* disprove the unscientific *theory* of evolution! I'm going to use my remaining seconds to say to Dr. Scott that if he cannot answer to our satisfaction what I have said, I will not leave this platform but will continue to stand here and point out his further fallacies." With that he stepped back.

The professor resumed his place at the podium. "I am not going," he intoned from reverberating speakers, "to be held hostage on this platform! Guards, remove this man!"

There were a few cries of *no* from the audience. "Let him stay!" hollered a woman.

A security man and a police officer were coming down the aisle as sporadic *boos* rolled over the scattered crowd and the empty seats.

"The people trusted you," Robert quietly said to the

professor. "You betrayed them. Their blood is on your hands."

"You're insane!"

The police officer stepped up on the platform and said, "I'm asking you to leave this auditorium."

"No, sir."

"Then you're under arrest. I charge you with disorderly conduct."

"My arrest will be the only orderly thing done here today." He held out his hands, and the officer snapped on the handcuffs. Robert stooped, picked up his case, and stepped off the platform to the sound of scattered applause as some of the people stood. He walked up the long aisle looking at the faces along the way and hearing the clapping stutter around the lecture hall. It was uphill, he told himself . . . like before, *When, in the course of human events, it becomes necessary . . . the laws of nature and of nature's God . . . they should declare the causes which impel them . . .*

Late that afternoon Dr. Allen Johnson phoned Robert at home and asked if he could meet him at his office again. He had tried, he said, to reach him since lunch, but asked if he could come now, because Carol had called about the seminar, and there were some things Robert needed to know. They briefly discussed the arrest, bail, and court date before hanging up. Beatrice said she would have a late dinner ready when he came back, and in the meantime she and the children would go grocery shopping.

"Carol called," said Dr. Johnson when Robert was seated in the little office as before, "during the first break after your arrest." Then he sat down in the other chair. He was wearing slacks and a sweater, which made him look more like a guy ready to take his wife out to eat than a gynecologist. "She said the seminar sort of went south after you left. The professor tried to use the situation to lambaste the ignorance of those who twist science the way he said you did, and someone in the audience demanded that he explain how evolution could have any basis of truth in light of the second law of thermodynamics. Carol said the guy with the question carried your argument further and got into entropy and laws of probability. The professor actually swore at the guy, and at that point some people got up and walked out. Then, the learned doctor began to rant about how evil in the world leaves no doubt concerning the validity of Darwin's conclusions. Someone then stood up and cited information from a biography of Charles Darwin that relates the part that philosophical problems concerning universal pain played in Darwin's formulation of his theory."

"Exactly," Robert responded. "Not many people know that Charles Darwin intended to go into the ministry before his voyage on the *Beagle*. Along the way he gave up his faith in the Bible and fell into the old trap of saying, 'If God is good, why does he allow suffering?' He forgot that Genesis clearly states—if he had just paid attention to simple words like *know*—that human beings said, in effect, 'We want to *know* evil.' And evil, of course, includes pain and suffering. Darwin forgot that God takes the human race more seriously than the human race takes God."

"Well," replied the other man, "Dr. Melvin Scott didn't have a very good day confronting the uninformed. However, there were some who agreed with the man fully and believe that he was severely mistreated, and they have vowed to make a big issue out of this."

"A big issue?"

"Yes. Carol said that there are some teachers and advisors around the state who believe that the American Civil Liberties Union is going to make everything right in this country, and they were saying that now is the time and this is the issue to bring intolerance to its knees."

"Intolerance! Christians are the ones who aren't being tolerated! Our rights are all but gone, and our vocabulary is treated the way pornography used to be treated!"

"They may make an issue of this, Robert. As I told you on the phone, there are some things you need to know—so you can make a decision."

"What things? What kind of decision?"

"For the last five years, I've been in contact with Senator Tave Perrin. As you know, Tave is powerful in Washington, and he's a Christian. One of the things Senator Perrin and his office have been involved in is a grass-roots attempt to get religious freedom back into this country. In short, he's very much aware of the influence and illegality of the government-sponsored religion of humanism. While Tave is a committed Christian, he sees the need for the real religious freedom our founding fathers worked, sacrificed, and sometimes, died for.

"Robert, what happened today at State University could be the drawing of a battle line. I feel sure the press will pick it up, and there will probably be some attention focused on you. You need to know that and be preparing for what might be coming."

"Which is?"

"I have no way of knowing for sure, but Tave's office has been working for five years, and there's a lot of people, all over the country, who are ready to line up behind the right person."

Robert raised his eyes to the painting: the sun golden on the haystack. Five years. "Why?" he asked. "Why did he start five years ago?"

"It had to start sometime."

Yeah, he thought in the silence that followed, then he said, "I'm just a schoolteacher, a fifth grade teacher—that's all. I don't want to lead anybody except my children."

The other man's eyes were on him, but he made no reply.

"I'm just a grade school teacher, that's all. I've got nothing to offer. Senator Perrin is known; he knows people, smart people—scientists, lawyers, doctors like you."

"Do you believe the Genesis account of creation, Robert?"

"Yes, of course."

"In the beginning, what did God have to work with?"

"Nothing."

The other man's eyes underlined the word's simple meaning.

Robert sat lost, he felt, somewhere in the past, or was it everywhere at once back there . . . on a shining day of not knowing where he was but trusting until a mirrored dawn came down in the west with silhouettes of places newly familiar like a curtain that had been blue over the stage of his life. "I'll be going," he said, "I need to get back to my—" He paused and almost smiled. "Could I ask you something?"

"Yes, of course."

"Would you be my best man?"

"Of course! When?"

"Soon. Perhaps very soon."

"Just let me know when, Robert. It will be a great honor."

"Oh, it'll be just a small wedding. There won't be many people, and the church building is small."

"It will be a great honor."

"Thank you."

They stood, shook hands, and Dr. Johnson said, "Thank you, Robert. For everything."

He nodded, touched the man's shoulder, and moved backward a couple of steps. A smile came quickly, he tossed a hand up in a partial wave, then he turned and walked briskly toward the outside door.

13

The sermon the next day was from the Old Testament book of Esther, one of two books in the Bible, said Pastor John, that does not mention God. "Yet," continued the man, "from our vantage point we see that our understanding of God's ordering of history—not just of the nation of Israel, but of all history—would be much less than it is without this book. Mordecai, Esther's guardian, said to her, 'who knows whether you have come to the kingdom for such a time as this?' That statement," said the pastor, "implies a purpose, unknown to man, of the unmentioned God. Esther was literally used to save the nation of Israel from slaughter. Without her, there would be no Israelites.

"Esther called for a fast, obviously for humility before the unmentioned God. She risked her life in breaking the law by going straight to the king. In this case she was in God's will and lived. Many others have been in God's will and died."

These words came to Robert flowing in among his memories, which they had called up, of Paula. They loosened and bore up pieces of sorrow so that some of the pieces seemed to float away in time's illusion. There was a purpose, he thought, as something like a haze departed too slowly to notice. Then it was gone—the misty haze—and the ocean sparkled in little waves laughing and bumping each other all around as far as could be seen, all the way out to where blue infinity came down to the water and gave it its blueness. And somewhere out there a little wooden chip rode bumping and sparkling along with a hickory leaf standing green in its laughing. That would be the purpose, he thought: redeeming nations, wood chips, and people from destruction. The purpose is to get all the family together with our Father for His glory. That's all.

When the service was over and almost everyone had gone, Robert and Beatrice approached the minister. Robert asked, "Would you have time next Saturday to do a small wedding?"

"Well," he answered as Robert expected he might, "I don't know. Who wants to get married?"

"They were in church today on the third pew. It was the man and woman with the two children."

Smiling broadly, the man extended his hand and they shook hands vigorously. "Congratulations, Robert! Of course, I'll do the wedding!"

"And," Robert added, "on Wednesday night, we want to invite the church family, and there's one other thing we'd like for you to do."

"I'll do it if I can."

"Well, you can certainly do this. Would you sing 'Wedding Song' for us—with your guitar?"

"I'd be happy to."

Robert turned to Beatrice and said, "No one who hears this man sing that song will ever forget it."

The pastor replied, "Beatrice will never forget the day anyhow."

"You're right," she said. "I'll never forget that day—if it ever comes!"

"It will," responded the minister. "The day of marriage . . . will come!"

Dr. Allen Johnson had been right. Sunday afternoon the phone at the Farr house rang as soon as they came in from church, and a reporter for *The Wardensville Watchman* wanted an interview with Robert. It would not be about yesterday's seminar, he said, but he wanted to do a human interest article on how it was that Robert had gotten into teaching. The focus would be, he said, upon the nuts and bolts of getting into the educational field with a view of helping young people who might be considering teaching as a career. Robert said, "Okay," giving Beatrice a nod as he did because she had been looking at him intently and listening to his side of the conversation to that point about a minute after the phone rang. He had said, "Hello," "Yes," and, "Okay," during that minute, but upon answering, he had put a hand over the receiver and mouthed, "Newspaper."

The reporter, Jimmy Dubbs, had a deadline, he said, so could he come over at two o'clock, he asked, an hour and fifteen minutes from now? Well, he might be able to make it later, but it would be a better article if he had that extra time to polish it before getting to his next assignment.

"Okay," Robert said again, then, "good-bye."

Beatrice put the baked chicken, creamed potatoes, and snap beans on the table in surprisingly short order. Robert's blessing included a request that the interview go well, and as they ate, he explained to Michael and Penny what had happened yesterday and why their father had been arrested. They stopped eating but resumed when he answered, no, he would not be going to jail, that this was a little bit like a game to remind people that if they don't stand up for what's right, wrong will take over. The newspaper reporter who was coming had a job to do, Robert told the children. His job was to print the truth so that people could form the right opinions and make the right decisions. The people, he said, will just about always make the right decisions if they are told the truth, and the Bible is the guidebook for truth because the Bible has never been shown to be wrong.

Yet, as he talked, Robert felt the discrepancy between the truth of the words he was saying and the reality that existed beyond the stone walls surrounding them. *The family,* he thought—*the last citadel,* as quietness came over them. Denominations have been infiltrated, many ministers have sold out to become waiters in social cafeterias called churches. He looked at the woman across the table—his wife in less than a week, and the mother of his children. She gave him a look, not as she had given when Allen the boy had said he would solve the puzzle, but a look that he could only describe as pregnant with hope. He reached out his hand, and she took it in the center of the table. She squeezed his hand very hard. Robert nodded, and they went back to eating, talking of other things: of how Sugar and Spice had gotten to know Michael and Penny and how the horses liked them a lot and would do what they said more often now than before. It had only rained one time yesterday, and that was fun because they had all gotten under an old wooden shed and kept dry, and Mom—Michael actually called her that—had said a prayer for Daddy. Robert thought that both he and Beatrice had been able to wipe their eyes without kids seeing. For a while that word was all he could think about.

Jimmy Dubbs came in with a camera, a notepad, and the manner of an old friend dropping by for a Sunday afternoon chat. He would run an occasional hand through his dark and shaggy hair as if to remind himself that after all, he was working and really should get back to the topic at hand, namely what do young people who are considering teaching as a career need to know about preparation? Should they be the patient type? Robert obviously had lots of patience and a great love of children. And it was super that Beatrice was here and wonderful that a love of children and teaching had been the common bond that brought them together, and he wished them the very best in marriage, and he would like to volunteer to take a few pictures after the wedding service and do a follow-up article in a few weeks.

Robert said they appreciated that but didn't want to be a bother, and they really didn't want publicity, but Mr. Dubbs would be welcome at the wedding. And the children, said Mr. Dubbs, were just wonderful. So sorry about Paula's death, but things certainly seemed to be working out. He took several pictures, closed his pad, and said that he really had to be getting on to his next assignment—a story about an elderly widow whose house was being condemned by the city.

They shook hands at the door, and Robert was holding it open for him when Jimmy Dubbs asked, "Robert—off the record—what happened at State University yesterday?"

Robert responded, "What have you heard?"

"Oh, just a bunch of loose ends about something like a debate at a schoolteachers' meeting."

"You did say this is off the record?"

"Absolutely! Whatever you say now is strictly off the record! See? I'm not making any notes."

"Well, there was a discussion about evolution and its impossibility."

"Sort of a replay of the 'Monkey Trial'?"

"You mean the Scopes Trial in Tennessee?"

"Yeah. That stuff got all settled then, as I recall."

"Not really. You see, evolution isn't true."

"You were arrested yesterday, weren't you?"

"Yes."

"Hmm. Sounds like a bunch of intolerant people—I mean, to have you arrested and all. Look, since you were arrested, there must be some major point you're trying go make. What is it?"

"Humanism is a religion, and it's the official state religion of our federal government. Humanism is aggressively propagated in the educational system of this country, and this is in clear violation of the First Amendment."

"And you're working against this?"

"Yes. I'm trying to make people aware that the First Amendment is being flagrantly violated by the state religion of humanism."

"How are you making people aware?"

"Any legitimate and legal way that I can. Situations like yesterday, letters—just getting the word out."

"I see! Well, good luck! I gotta run. Thanks for your time, and the best to you in your marriage!" They shook hands again, and Jimmy Dubbs hurried down the walk to his car.

Robert closed the door and encountered Beatrice's eyes. "I think," he said, "that the word is about to get out big time."

"Yes. I wondered if you knew that."

"Beatrice." He gave a little grin. "Just how simple do you think I am?"

"You're a Christian, Robert. And sometimes real Christians become very vulnerable."

"To what?"

She looked at the closed door and so did he. There it was, standing out as it does from so many doors. "The word," she said quietly, "is . . . the *cross*."

The next day Dr. Allen Johnson phoned the school and left word for Robert to call him whenever he had a few minutes to talk. At first recess, Robert called, identified himself, and in a few seconds the doctor was on the phone saying they needed to get together again and could Robert come at four? Four-thirty would be better, he explained, because he and a certain lady needed to buy some rings. Four-thirty it was, and as Robert hung up the phone, Carol came in the outside office and motioned with her head toward her private office. He went in, she followed, closed the door, told him to have a seat, then walked over and sat down at her desk. Her face had the same lack of expression as that day at the law office when he first went in, and he knew this was because of the door's window and the glass wall. "I asked Beatrice to take your class for a while when they come from recess," she said in a low voice. "You're getting a good woman." She glanced down at her desk as if she were consulting notes, but there was nothing in front of her except the beige blotter.

"Thank you," he replied almost belatedly.

"Don't," she responded with raised eyes and a slightly elevated voice, "thank me! I don't want that. You once told me—" Now her head came up. "—that you didn't want anything from me. Well—there's something I want from you—just one thing."

"What's that?"

"Two transfers. You and Beatrice. Out of here."

"Okay."

"I can arrange it. Where would you like to go?"

"Nowhere."

"What do you mean, nowhere?"

"I'm through with public schools. No way, no more. Beatrice and I are going to wait and try to get in at Shadley."

"I'm sorry to hear that. You're very good. But it seems the good are getting out . . . of everything."

"You know, I'm still confused. I don't want to sit here and list all the things you've called me, all the times you—"

"Robert—knock, knock! Is anyone home in your head? Do I have to spell it out? For a guy who's so sharp, you can be so dense! Evidence, Bobby-boy! Evidence! You set yourself up as evidence, and I examined you."

"I didn't mean to set myself up. I was just trying—"

"That—you are! Look, Robert—this is *my* fault, okay? I'm a grown woman who knows how to play, and I've played this game before, but—"

"You call it a game?! Carol—what in the world—"

"Robert—just stop! Don't say anymore! Just go on back to . . . your class and your virgin-pure bride . . . and have a good life! Go *some*where and live happily ever after!"

"Why did you call her that?"

"Because that's what she is."

"Is that wrong?"

Carol sprang to her feet with a fist to the desk, emphasizing each word, "*No!* no, that's *not* wrong!" She paused, glancing at the ceiling. Then she looked at him, shaking her head back and forth, and said softly, "It's *not* wrong." She took a deep breath and sat down. "You can be very trying," she added.

"I'm sorry."

"Would you quit saying that? Why do you always apologize?"

"I'm not apologizing. Most of the time when I say that, what I mean is that I'm sad."

"Well, don't be—for me."

"Okay."

She gave him an exasperated look and shook her head again, causing her hair to swing back and forth under her chin. In her not telling him they had nothing else to talk about, he realized that this might be one of last times they would talk like this, or talk at all. She would choose the time, and Carol wasn't the type who waited around. Their eyes were locked as they had been across the auditorium, and she was telling him things with them that she would never say with that beautiful mouth. Some of them were little girl things, and some of them were woman things— man and woman things—and even though he and Beatrice were going to buy the rings today . . . He was even now making a choice, a decision, as the word *war* fleeted through his mind. And it was a war, but it was not seeming so wrong now, after all. Consenting adults. Not children. As something in a dream, the war was becoming a game, a game more important than the war. Carol had said she didn't lose . . . Carol would not push away or say no.

"Robert Farr, you're made of stone."

"What?" he said, feeling the sound too sudden and blurted.

"Nothing." She looked away and sort of admitted defeat with her face.

Something was pounding, and Robert listened to the trip-hammer dropping to why-I-shouldn't. Another minute . . . was shaking him inside . . . and he would have lost everything . . . but not in this room with a glass wall. Maybe in going out he might have realized and stopped. Maybe, maybe not. And that scared him like she had always said he was scared. Beatrice even said he was scared, and Robert knew he was—so much that he needed to say something, but he didn't know what. She still wasn't looking at him, so he said her word, "Nothing."

Carol turned her eyes on him.

"Could be the name of anything."

She looked back as before, and at length said, "Yeah—" Then, "You always were good with words."

"But there was one—that didn't fit."

"Which one was that?"

"Molester."

"Don't worry about that."

"Why not?"

"There's not going to be any evidence—for that."

"Carol—" Their eyes locked, and he said, "Thank you."

"Thank me? For what?"

"For—perhaps what you would call nothing."

"Robert, did anyone ever tell you that you're strange? Or does that come from always getting everything you ever wanted?"

"Not everything I ever wanted, my dear, but everything I ever needed."

She was smiling. "I love you."

"I know."

The smile diminished but remained, and she whispered, "Robert—"

"And, as a Christian—"

"I know—"

"I love you."

The sounds from the outside office softened under their

silence as the world quietens under a deep and heavy snow at night when the only stars are swarming to earth from somewhere above a street light not far away. Finally, Carol said, "Well—" and the word floated upon that stillness until, "I guess we've said everything . . . that needs saying . . . except—" She turned the chair slightly, and there was a little squeak. "I'm going to take two or three days off this week and next week. Things are sort of slow, and Eunice can handle it. We might not see each other again except at a distance, and—I've got a replacement for you—anytime after today."

"I'd like to finish the week."

"I thought you would. That's fine. Beatrice?"

"That's up to you."

"Whatever she wants to do." Carol got up and walked leisurely over to the corner behind him. "Robert—" she said softly. He turned his head but could not see her. "Come here." He stood and faced her. "Are you still afraid, even now?"

"Yes."

"Come here."

She was standing where no one could see from the outer office. He hesitated, took a couple of steps, and stopped. A little smile touched her lips, but she said nothing. He had no thoughts now as such; he continued to look at her, then he moved and her face was turned up to his inches away. Her soft fingers caressed his face, then she kissed him. His hands went to her shoulders; he drew her closer without really meaning to. Carol stopped and just looked at him, smiled and whispered, "So—you're not made of stone!" She moved back a step and quietly said, "Recess is over." Straightening his tie, she added, "It's not polite to keep a lady waiting." She turned, and with an extended arm, opened the door, then stood there with her palm up in an invitation for him to leave. "Don't worry," she whispered, "she'll never notice the lipstick!"

A little dazed, Robert went out, passed Dunstal with his face burning, and a few seconds later was walking down the hall imagining Carol's lipstick all over his mouth. He hurried into a restroom and checked his face in the mirror: there was not a trace of lipstick. For some reason he put a couple of fingers on his mouth and closed his eyes. Carol's perfume was on his hands.

CHAPTER

14

That afternoon Robert sat in Dr. Allen Johnson's waiting room with the little box containing two rings in his coat pocket. He felt some remorse that there had been no engagement ring, but Beatrice did not want one. She said she had spent a year being engaged before and nothing had come of it. Was it really remorse over the ring or regret over the fact that he had not known her longer, he wondered as he shifted in the chair. There was no hesitation about getting married on the part of either of them, but still, things were happening so fast. Yet a long courtship, as his parents called what they had had, doesn't necessarily make a good marriage; that they had demonstrated.

Now at his first opportunity to sit down and think about Carol at her office door today, he was more sure than ever about the wedding. Carol was, too, by the way she had held the door open and the look she had given him. It seemed that she ..

"Mr. Farr—"

"Yes." He got up and followed the receptionist down the hall to the office with the haystacks by Monet.

"Dr. Johnson will be right in," said the woman as she turned and almost bumped into the doctor coming in the room.

When they were seated, Dr. Johnson asked, "Have you seen the newspaper article?"

"No, I'd nearly forgotten."

The man took a clipped article from the chest pocket of his white jacket, handed it to Robert, and said, "Typical media."

Above a picture of Robert and Beatrice sitting on the couch with Michael and Penny was the large-lettered caption: 'Local teacher arrested, girds to take on Uncle Sam.' Robert jerked his head up and said, "This is ridiculous!"

"Read on, the best is yet to come!"

He put his glasses on and began to read:

Robert Farr is angry, and Robert Farr is not going to take it anymore! Picture this: a quiet educational gathering in tranquil Kaiser Hall on State campus . . . a mundane lecture about evolution . . . suddenly Robert Farr, a former U.S. Marine with firsthand experience in the savage violence that was Vietnam charges the stage and disrupts an elderly professor, virtually pushing the man away from his podium.

"This is all lies!" Robert exclaimed loudly, starting to rise from the chair.

"I know, but calm down and read it."

He glanced out the door and resumed the article aloud. "'Finally, Farr, a self-appointed crusader against big government, was arrested, handcuffed, and taken away. The crowd mostly resented Farr's intrusion and applauded his arrest.' Lies!" Robert said, and the gut knot came back hurting. "The guy said everything about the seminar was off the record! I thought he would mention it, but not—"

"Robert—to a reporter, there's no such thing as 'off the record.' Frankly, I expected a little stretching of the truth, but I never expected anything like this! Now, there's a reason why you don't need to be too upset about this, and I'll tell you that reason when you finish the article."

He read silently to near the end when the words again were forced into sound. "'Farr has two children by a previous marriage, and Beatrice Bertram, his current girlfriend, seems to totally share his belief and life-style. Keep your eye on Robert Farr. He's out to bring down what he sees as government-sponsored religion: humanism, he calls it. (Ever seen a humanist? Well, neither have I.) Farr is an old-fashioned gunslinger jumping stages on his way to the big showdown in the sky.'" Robert fell limply back in the chair and removed the glasses.

"Now," said Dr. Johnson, "I never in my wildest dreams expected such blatant cheap shots! If I had, I would have certainly warned you much more than I did! But when all is said and done, that article may be a very good thing."

He fixed a vacant stare on the man's face. "How?"

"Tave Perrin. For five years the man has organized and worked and gotten ready. He's got a small army of lawyers, media experts, and people who have been waiting for a visible situation where the other side makes a mistake and goes too far. Of course, both sides have been doing the same thing, and it looks like time will show that the battle line was drawn here."

"But, I didn't want all this. I just wanted to get on with my life, that's all I wanted."

"You also said you wanted to 'petition the Government for a redress of grievances.'"

"Yes," he answered wearily, "I did say that, and I'm going to do it—with every ounce of strength I have."

"All we're after is religious freedom, Robert. That's all. America as we have known her is dying internally, simply because the eternal truths of the Bible have been forgotten. In 1892, the Supreme Court ruled that 'this is a Christian nation' in the case of the Church of The Holy Trinity versus The United States. Today, less than one hundred years later, Christians are routinely harassed, persecuted, and ridiculed. And this is just the beginning!"

"Allen, not much is ever said about the part Darwinism played in the formulation of Adolf Hitler's philosophy. The concept of the 'super race' rests completely on survival of the fittest, and Hitler viewed Jews and Negroes as 'missing links.' And that's scary because so many educated people were deceived.

"The thing that scares me the most," continued Robert, "is something Carol said—that people don't want to know the truth, that they don't care. I'm afraid that's true. People are intimidated. However, if the American people were asked privately if they approved of homosexuality, nearly every person would shout no! The majority of Americans are against abortion on demand and our tax money supporting the practice. Most Americans want prayer in the schools and at other public gatherings. The great majority of Americans don't agree with the way our schools are being run. Most of us strongly object to being led down the road to socialism and the welfare state. We don't agree with the brand of politics that seems intent on relegating us to a second- or third-rate power. What happened to 'consent of the governed'?"

"It's the responsibility of the governed to get it back."

"What's Senator Perrin's plan?"

"I sent a fax of the newspaper article to his office. He's going to call me tonight. I think he'll say that this is the time to make a beginning."

"You know something?" Robert said. "I was actually worried about meeting with the school board! Now, that meeting is out of the picture, and it seems like small potatoes!"

Allen replied, "Another interesting factor about all this is Carol—and even Cyrus. They both have called me, and neither one knows about the other's calling. I think that slowly, some of Carol's basic assumptions about the Bible are beginning to break up. You'll never guess what she asked me."

"What?"

"If I could recommend a good Bible dictionary."

Robert looked up at the painted haystacks . . . at the pinkish and golden half-colors. "Good." He smiled. "That's—very good!"

"And Cyrus said, 'You know, this Farr guy is right! If he needs me to go to bat for him, just let me know!'"

Robert looked at the other man. "I'm—really surprised—"

"Why?"

"I—I don't know—really. Why I should be . . . surprised."

"I don't either."

There was a pause, then Allen said, "You asked about Senator Perrin's plan."

"Yes."

"Tave has access to some influential people. There are plans for a group of about one to two hundred Christians from all over the country who have been seriously harassed and/or persecuted to meet in Washington, D.C., on March twenty-fourth. That's the Friday before Easter. Tave is making arrangements for a few from this group to speak personally to some top officials, possibly even the president. There is to be a brief prayer vigil at the Supreme Court Building and then a march to several other locations for interviews and the presentation of signed petitions. Not every person in government is on the other side—some are serious Christians. I feel sure that Senator Perrin will want you at least to be present. Do you think you can go?"

"Yes."

"I'll tell him that tonight. Do you have any qualms about talking personally with high officials?"

"No."

"Good. And, Robert—I think the newspaper article is going to help us a lot. Don't worry about it."

"I'm not. But I do regret the implications that I might be divorced and living with Beatrice without being married."

"I believe Mr. Dubbs and *The Watchman* are going to deeply regret that article and *all* its implications."

"Well, I don't mean to change the subject, but—"

"Yes?"

"We're thinking about a two o'clock wedding this Saturday. Is that a good time for you?"

"Yes, indeed."

"And you know where the church is?"

"Oh, yes."

"And—just a suit—nothing formal."

"I'm looking forward to it."

Robert smiled. "So am I! And, you know what?"

"What?"

"I met Beatrice's parents for a little while this past Saturday, after I was arrested! She and her parents have a tremendous relationship. She had already explained everything to them. You wouldn't believe what her father said." The other man was becoming blurred, but Robert continued on undaunted, "Her father said, 'Well done. All we've ever wanted—all these years—was for Daniel to come back home.' Daniel was their son who was killed in Nam. Mr. and Mrs. Bertram said their son believed in this country, and they would be ashamed for him to know some things about it now. They said Beatrice told them that Daniel and I were very much alike in our beliefs. Her parents hugged me and cried. They said Beatrice had found them another son. You see—my middle name is Daniel." Robert paused and then stood. "I have to go. They invited me over for dinner tonight."

⊡

The newspaper article was the talk of the school. Connelly smiled each time she saw Robert, a smile of derision as if to say that justice was finally about to fall on the obnoxious cause of all her personal failures and disappointments. He spoke kindly to her the first time he saw her after the article came out, and she cursed at him; after that she put on the smile whenever they met.

The other teachers mostly avoided him, and when there were two or more of them together, they ignored him, talking to each other and acting for all the world as if Robert did not exist. When he encountered a teacher by herself, she would take a deep breath and look down. Stacy Robertson and Eunice Phillips were the only ones who did speak to him; the others that he tried to talk with did not respond. Maybe, Robert told Beatrice at lunch one day, this was the reason—more than any other—that Carol had taken the days off. Carol, as she had often said, knew her people.

But the class was different. The children looked at him more, probably recalling what parents and other grown-ups had said; beyond that, for most of them, it was business as usual. A few parents stopped by the school or called him at home to thank him for the stand he was taking. They said they knew what had really happened at the seminar, that most people knew and that a lot of letters were being written to the newspaper complaining about the article. *The Capitol City Conveyor*, the largest newspaper in the state, carried an account about Robert's arrest on State campus, and the thrust of its report was a little more factual. However, his position was said to be representative of "an archaic segment of every society that is always behind the eight ball of time." A national news agency picked up the account as a single paragraph with the lead sentence, "A new David and Goliath sport has come to an NCAA campus."

Beatrice was also shunned, though not as fully as Robert, and they talked a time or two about how some other religions also occasionally make use of the practice. She said that Connelly had told her in the lounge that Robert was ruined and that she would personally see to that. She apparently hadn't expected Beatrice's reaction—a step forward, and "Well, have at it!" After that there were no smiles or anything else directed at Beatrice from anyone.

The bright spot of the week had been Wednesday night at church when immediately following Robert's invitation to the wedding, the pastor gave him an envelope containing 253 dollars. This was the church's gift to be used toward a honeymoon, he said, and after that, Mr. Swenson stood up and said that he and his wife would keep Michael and Penny for as long as the honeymoon might last, and the longer the better. There was laughter and applause, and Robert said, "Thank you," swallowed hard, and sat down.

The last two days of the school week went much like the first three, until Friday afternoon. On that day Robert and Beatrice brought refreshments for his class, and they had a party, a "moving on party," he called it. Stacy and Eunice were invited; and they came, watching, as he had asked them to, while he took each child in turn on his knee and hugged him or her, saying special things that each needed to hear—things that Eunice and Stacy also heard. The tears of most of the children he wiped away with the paper towels Eunice had brought and put on the desk. He used one or two of the towels himself, and then—the children were gone.

The bell had rung, and the day—the class day—was over. The room and the hall had gone silent, and Stacy and Eunice had gone—after hugging him and turning away with their tears. Silence kept ringing like a bell, and Beatrice alone leaned on it and on the desk as she looked out the window. Her back was to him, and her hair. He loved her and this room and even the halls. And the cedar tree where Natasha had put the bird . . . and cried. Her crayon drawing he had given to her parents. The circle with everything in it of the world tilted on the desk beside Beatrice's hand.

Robert stood and walked slowly to the back of the room to stand beside the desk where he had sat the day Robert the student gave his descriptive summary. The desk was small and scarred . . . and old. He had not paid much attention to how old.

How's Jefferson Elementary's best male teacher?
Stuck. How do you get out of one of these things?
You learn not to get in in the first place.
The first place? That was a long time ago. I could fit in then.

He turned and looked the length of the room into her eyes. The silence held them both unmoving in that moment. Impressions came carouselling: smells of fresh air and body odor swirled around the laughter, pushing, and the wire spiral of the grade book in the top drawer of the desk . . hurting . . . more than his fingers in their squeezing. Boys swathed in bloody bandages and dying . . . calling Mama. Michael had called her Mom. Mom . . . ironing and nodding with her eyes to him about this very minute that she could not have known—any more than Carol could know about the jungle—And this minute called life, that children know and grown-ups call death.

Leaving, going home . . . "Let's go home," he said, and he wondered where it was with that old wondering like the day with her and the children when they came in from under the sky to sit down at the table and eat together. He walked to her and held out his hand. She took it and held it to her face, and he looked at the doorway where she had stood waiting that day before she had become more than a name coming to him through the darkness. With their arms around each other, they went to the door. Beatrice stepped into the hall, and without looking back, Robert reached around and closed the door quietly behind them.

"Dearly beloved—we are gathered here today in the presence of God and before the face of this company to join together this man and this woman in holy matrimony," Pastor John was saying. Other than his voice, a hush prevailed over the forty people crowded into the little church building. Between the sentences and some of the words, silences came to join all that had gone before with what Robert could only call the moving and mysterious now and the wonder that was happening in it. "Marriage is instituted of God, and signifies unto us the mystical union that is between Christ and His church. This holy estate, Christ adorned and beautified with His presence and first miracle . . .

"Who giveth this woman to be married to this man?"

"Her mother and I."

Veiled in white beside him with the strength of her hands interlocking his, her heartbeat was there and he could feel it as his own. Her smile of knowing became an incredible gift more beautiful than he had ever seen or imagined, and as she squeezed his hand, words fled away that might have described what he saw in the sparkling depth of her eyes beneath that veil.

"Robert Farr, wilt thou take this woman to be thy lawfully wedded wife? Wilt thou love her, honor, protect, and cherish her, and forsaking all others, keep thee only unto her so long as ye both shall live?"

"I do."

"Beatrice Bertram, wilt thou take this man to be thy lawfully wedded husband? Wilt thou love him, honor and obey him, and forsaking all others, keep thee only unto him so long as ye both shall live?"

"I do."

"The rings are symbols," the pastor said, ". . . precious . . . endless . . ."

Their hands joined again; and the golden bands on their fingers Robert held up so that Allen Johnson and Pastor John could see, so the bridesmaid could see, and in their smiles he refused the shout that he wanted so much to give with all his ecstatic soul. He turned slightly to the side and held their hands before the faces of Michael and Penny standing like a wise man and an angel, lost in the wonder of the grace of God in giving gifts to man. The children hesitated, glanced up at their faces, and then their small hands reached out to touch the rings as if to handle all that had come about to forever change their lives. There was no voice that could be heard in those moments of touching and lingering fingers, but there was the voice that Robert knew and felt as perhaps those present at the first miracle knew and felt: *Well done—*

The pastor offered a prayer of thanksgiving, then held out two small pieces of bread; Robert and Beatrice took them and stood beholding the fragments in their fingers as the minister continued. "Jesus said, 'Take, eat; this is My body, which is broken for you; this do in remembrance of Me.'"

They ate the bread, then he offered one small cup, which they both took and held. Pastor John again said, "Jesus said, 'This cup is the new testament in My blood: this do ye, as oft as ye drink it, in remembrance of Me.' " Robert drank first, then Beatrice, and they handed the cup back. The man placed it on the table behind him and took up his guitar, leaning there on a stand.

"God gives gifts to humans," he said, putting the leather strap over his shoulder. "One of these gifts is song. Song involves order, harmony, and purpose. Long ago, minstrels traveled about the countryside singing songs to people who would gather to hear them. It's interesting that the word *minstrel* comes from the root word *minister*, and minister means *servant*. These minstrels were known as troubadours from the French word *trobar*, which means 'to compose in verse.' One of the basic purposes of a minister is to help people compose their lives in the order, harmony, and purpose of Jesus Christ, the resurrected Son of God. So, to some extent, I suppose that a minister is a troubadour. As a troubadour, I'll sing for you now—acting on the part of the God who became flesh and was crucified, and yet lives and moves within us as the church."

The clear notes of the guitar rang out, then the voice of the man arose like that day of blue sky and fields weaving together:

He is now to be among you At the calling of your hearts Rest assured, this troubadour is acting on His part. The union of your spirits here has caused Him to remain. For whenever two or more of you are gathered in His name There is love, there is love.

The order and the harmony came from the singing strings as his fingers touched the moving notes with purpose.

Well, a man shall leave his mother And a woman leave her home They shall travel on to where the two shall be as one As it was in the beginning, is now And 'til the end Woman draws her life from man and gives it back again And there is love, there is love.

The guitar lifted an interlude, a rest from singing but not from hearing, with the children standing close beside her so that he could see them and her veiled face.

The marriage of your spirits here has caused Him to remain For whenever two or more of you are gathered in His name, There is love, there is love.

The notes rose up and receded, and the song was over, but not the memory. And the silence following . . .

"Forasmuch as Robert and Beatrice have consented together in holy wedlock . . . I now pronounce that they are husband and wife. What God has joined together, let not man put asunder."

Robert lifted the veil and kissed his wife.

Over the next few minutes, the people began gravitating through a door behind and slightly to the left of the pulpit. There was a lot of hand shaking and slapping of backs. Mrs. Swenson's portly efforts at the piano splendored up against the rising clamor of voices saying nothing discernible unless someone had an ear in front of someone else's mouth, whether by choice or by chance. The woman finally acknowledged the rout of her keyboard entry into chaos with a broad smile and raised hands. She stood and left the seat like a hen satisfied with the laying of an egg. Her arms flew around the person nearest her, and then another, until, like a chant, people began to pick up on embracing—one or two literally. The diminutive Widow Puckett was taken up in a couple of elevated, straitjacket-type spins that left her straw hat awry with its two silk daisies pointing out to the sides like antennae. Upon coming down and being released, the little lady jabbed a slow-motion punch at the ceiling like Bucky Thornton, a basketball star at State.

The confusion was spilling down the back hall and into a room the size of a basketball half court known as the fellowship hall. Heads bobbed along over a flood of shoulders and the smells of shaving lotions as laughing voices now swirled loudly only to fall to subdued whispers. Bright, darting eyes took in everything. These eyes and hands and shoulders had come together last night to ready the building—it was their sweat, provided by their God in the first place, that had done these things, and it was His love alone that provided all things, and it was as if now they were carrying Him along on their shoulders in thanksgiving.

At the double-wide door to the fellowship hall, on the right, the crowd spread itself out into little groups and individuals standing around or sitting in chairs along the far wall. What was left of a receiving line was coming to an end; everyone knew there was no need to stand in line to pump Robert's hand again, but they would anyhow—so that no more than four at a time would be waiting to pump, embrace, wipe their eyes, or say something special that they had planned. Flash bulbs going off reminded him of a movie he had once seen where an electric transformer was blown up at the end, at night, and the hero's face had reflected alternating volumes of light so that he appeared both triumphant and scared in successive measures. There was no sign of Mr. Jimmy Dubbs or his camera, but Robert and Beatrice certainly had not counted on him anyway. Pete Smith was something like the church's resident photographer, and some of those flashes were coming from the bright ball of light floating around where his chest and head should be.

Most people were eating from glass plates they held in their hands or rested on their knees, or drinking from matching glass cups that fit into a circular ridge near the edge of each plate. Duffy Hutchins, a widower, had insisted in many church business meetings that plates with such cup holders be bought because his cups never stayed put. Finally, when the score was plates 70, cups 35, his motion was passed with the amendment that the new serving sets be called "the Duffy-proof stuff." Someone had given Robert a Duffy cup, and he sipped the cold, green punch amid handshakes and talking. The ice crystals between his teeth felt like a boy walking on new snow, and if he had had time to close his eyes, he might have gone by that street light again with all the stars swarming to earth in that cold and cozy fragment of a memory.

Finally, the cake had been cut and greatly diminished. Robert had taken the garter from Beatrice's calf and tossed it up over his shoulder and down into the sure hands of Duffy Hutchins, who appeared disoriented by the jeers, cheers, whistles, and clapping that reddened his face and broadened his grin. "Hey, Duffy," a man shouted, "how come you didn't drop *that*?!"

Duffy reached over and squeezed Robert's bicep. "Because—it's Duffy-proof!" The people roared in laughter.

Next, the single women gathered for the tossing of the bouquet. Beatrice stepped back, then forward like a quarterback—drawing cheers from the men as the bouquet turned over slowly just under the ceiling in an arching flight of green and store-bought spring flowers bound by a hand-wrapped white ribbon—tied by some of the very hands reaching up toward it now. Suddenly the reaching hands withdrew and a path opened to a diminutive old woman wearing a straw hat with daisies sticking out on the sides like antennae. A light seemed to flash down on her wrinkled face, turning it into a instantaneous smile, and her hands went up with gnarled fingers extended toward the falling prize. The bouquet revolved once more and then settled into her hands with fingers curling gently into the flowers. Mrs. Puckett held it there where it had been caught—for a heartbeat—then she pulled it to her chest and bowed her head. She looked up quickly with glassy eyes, and then again threw a slow-motion fist toward the ceiling. The applause and cheering in the room was deafening.

Now—Robert knew—was the time; two young girls appeared on either side of the door to the outside with baskets in their hands. There was a stirring in the little crowd, a swirl of excitement and a movement that brought the children first and then the older ones toward the door. A child reached into one of the baskets and withdrew a little measure of rice tied up in a piece of pink netting. "Just one," a woman said, and then other hands were plunging into the baskets, and Pete Smith opened the door and adjusted the stay at the top to hold it open. The line of people spilled out and down the two steps to the ground, casting themselves into near silhouettes in the doorway while Robert and Beatrice stood alone in the center of the room. He took her hand and wondered . . . No, she wouldn't be thinking of Daniel . . . she was a woman and couldn't know. Lines of white chutes popping out like flowers in a blue field. Standing as if on green velvet far below. *Stand up. Hook up. Stand in the door—*

He and she stood in the door looking down at the people ready to throw. In a moment, their eyes joined, and he kissed her lips before them all, forgetting those who were watching . . . waiting. He breathed her fragrance and her breath and felt her hair beneath his hand as his fingers curled gently into its softness.

Again there was cheering and applause, and a man hollered something about not much longer to wait. They looked down at them and waved with their hands high. Michael and Penny were standing with Beatrice's parents with their rice ready. The Swensons understood; they were grandparents themselves, and there would be another time for them to keep the children.

Then Robert and Beatrice were running and ducking and laughing and being showered with rice. Her car had been readied with shaving cream and tin cans tied to the rear bumper. They jumped in, Robert put the key into the ignition and started the car; so far, so good. They drove away waving, and three cars followed, blowing horns and blinking headlights. The cars followed all the way to the farm, and when Robert turned down the long lane to the house, the cars left them—miraculously, Robert said.

They changed clothes; he cleaned up the car and put their suitcases in the trunk. Before getting in for the drive to the beach, he looked at the house and said, "You know—no one is going to be here for several days, and—"

"No," she said. "And that's the last no I'll ever say to you."

He shrugged. "Do you mean if I were to ask again, you'd say yes?"

"Yes, but—"

"But what?"

"I think the cars would come back."

"Then get in," he said, opening her door for her.

Beatrice complied with something of a quizzical look. Robert closed the door, went around the car, and got in. He backed along the lane nearly to the road where he got out and closed the gate. In the car again, he drove back to the house where he parked in the backyard so the car could not be seen from the road. He bounced out and guided her quickly around to the front door where he opened it, scooped her up in his arms, and carried her inside. With his shoulder he closed the door behind them.

Prismed droplets of rainbowing ocean spray leaping in joy ... ecstatically flowing, then receding: white, foamy lines on golden sand ... all under the bluest of cloudless warm breezes coming down around them ruffling their hair and filling their ears, but when the other spoke ... not noticed. White curling in falling blueish emerald ... when she told him after hardly more than a week that she thought—no she just *knew* ...

Oh, that men would give thanks to the LORD *for His goodness, and for His wonderful works to the children of men!*

Sun scattered on the things of its shining, living and

green, and without it for a time: nothing. At just the right angle tilted toward her hand. And the circle containing all the things of his days—out front by the door—when it rains.

The hay, golden, pink, and yellow, all harvested and stacked up in diffusion of light broken down by effects of itself on the straw and the world . . . in its wonder.

"Hello, Robert," said the voice of a man behind him. "Did you find that the moon is made of honey?"

"Yes," he answered, still standing and looking at the painting. "It's honey—not cheese. The theory was wrong."

"I see."

"I know. But many don't."

There came a silence that he finally turned around in to see Allen Johnson standing, now looking like a doctor. There was a pause, then the man nodded toward the chair by the wall where he would usually sit and said, "You look very good, Robert, very good, indeed! Please have a seat."

They sat down and Robert couldn't restrain a smile at the other man's puzzling look. "It's like I'm a new man, isn't it?"

"Well—yes. You look and seem so rested and at ease."

"Allen—" Robert waited after saying the man's name for a time to gather up the words to say what he felt, but on a joyous impulse, he plunged in. "These last few weeks have been the best days of my life! That's not taking anything away from my marriage to Paula—what I'm saying is that all the goodness of those years was added to . . . during these last days—sort of continued under high concentration and high magnification—listen to me!" He grinned to a stop. "It was wonderful! Better than I ever imagined! We walked up and down the beach, went to shops, performances—did the ordinary things that people do when they go there—but everything was so intense—intensely relaxing, is what I'm trying to say . . . I mean—"

"You mean you're in love."

"Yes! It's wonderful, Allen. Look, even when we sit down together to eat, it's tremendous just being together. And you know what? You'll never guess—and it happened *during* the honeymoon—"

"During the honeymoon? What could that be? What could possibly happen during a honeymoon that I would know anything about?"

"Beatrice is pregnant."

Dr. Johnson's smile was response enough for Robert, but the man added, "I'm very happy, Robert—very happy indeed."

"Thank you! It's—well, it's wonderful!"

"There's a gift that I'd like to give."

"A gift?"

"Yes. My services."

Robert's gaze went to the painted stacks of hay while behind his eyes he saw again the beam of sunlight sloping down into the trough onto a little impression in the hay, bathing it in gold. He could have done better than a stable. "I don't understand," Robert half whispered, "I don't understand . . . at all—"

"You don't understand what?"

"His love." There was silence, then Robert said, "Thank you. Thank you . . . very much."

There came another silence.

"Well—" said Robert as he turned to the doctor wondering why he called, "that's all I have."

"I called," responded the other man, "because a few things have come up. Have you read your mail since you got back?"

"No, we came home, heard your message on the answering machine, and I called here. I haven't gone by the post office yet to get the mail."

"Well, I've gotten a couple of calls from Senator Perrin in the last two days. The letters you sent out apparently have gotten some responses. At least, Tave said his office has heard about them. He said a member of the state house contacted him and said the mail-out has been something of a wake-up call to a few people in his area."

"Have there been negative responses?"

"Not that I've heard about . . . to the letters. But Tave said that a lot more people than he ever thought would be there are going to be there day after tomorrow. Another similar organization has come in, and they want to get in on the petitions and the march. He's anticipating between two and three thousand people."

"That's great! But the letters couldn't have caused all this."

"No, the letters had nothing to do with the other group coming in; this conflict isn't new. Now—what I wanted to tell you is this: Tave has learned that at least two socialist-extremist groups are going to have people there. These organizations—now, get this—get some backing from, and include in their membership, some individuals in government and in the national media!"

"I'm not surprised."

"Nor am I—not in the least. But it seems that the word has gotten around that there's likely to be some violence this Friday, the twenty-fourth, instigated by the extremist groups."

"Is the word reliable?"

"Tave's taking it seriously enough to have asked for a small army of police officers to be on hand."

Robert looked away to the far wall, not far away at all in this little room. Almost able to be touched just by reaching out, and all snow white across the desk . . .

"Robert?"

Their eyes met, and Allen Johnson asked, "Would you like to ride up to D.C. with me tomorrow afternoon? I've made reservations in a motel not far out of town."

"Yes. I'd like to do that."

"Good. I'll call you about what time we'll need to leave."

"Okay. And thanks . . . for everything."

"Sure," Dr. Johnson grinned. "Look, when we get back, let's take Saturday off and go fishing."

"It's a deal! Boy, has it been a long time! And we could take my son, Michael, if you don't mind. He'd really love it."

"By all means! I know just the place . . . stocked with lunkers! We can go anytime—courtesy of a patient's appreciative husband."

"Great!" They stood. "See you tomorrow."

"See you then, Robert."

The Washington Monument at night was a far off golden needle pointing straight up into a velvety springtime sky. Robert took the compass from his pocket and walked a short distance from the open door of the motel and stood under a streetlight, watching its needle quivering toward magnetic north. The city's lights made it impossible to see any stars, but he looked up anyway at a vapor of light thrown up under the blackness. Michael and Penny would be in bed by now—Penny with her teddy bear, and Michael was probably looking up at the dark wedge on the wall that was the Shadley Shamrocks' pennant. Beatrice would be in his bed in the stone house; they would start moving furniture Monday to the farmhouse. And once again, the old Shannon house would be up for sale.

Dad, would you bring me a Senator's baseball pennant?
Sure will.
And a blade of grass, said Penny, *from the White House lawn?*
Well, if the guards don't mind, he had said into the telephone receiver.
Then Beatrice had said, *I love you, Robert.*
I love you—
I'll be waiting—
Neither he nor Allen had said anything to their wives about possible violence. He turned lightheartedly and walked back into the motel room and closed the door. His suit, tie, and the nice white shirt Penny had given him for

his birthday were all hanging on the rack awaiting the wake-up call.

Robert read Psalm 107, and Allen prayed. They said good night, and each man got into his bed. In a few minutes it seemed like the doctor was snoring, but it must have been a breeze, because Robert was walking along the beach again with his arm around his wife, and they were laughing because they were very happy.

Across the bottom of the pediment of the massive white marble building that looked like a Greek temple were the words *EQUAL JUSTICE UNDER LAW*. But things had gotten ugly, and it wasn't working out that way. A pregnant woman crumpled and lay unmoving on the bottom step in a pool of blood. There was screaming and cursing, and a man went sprawling under the spattering glass from a flying bottle. Barricades wavered, then crashed to the street, and men spilled over. Some had metal pipes. Screams and chaos swirled in profusion, then came the staccato echoing thunder of automatic weapons. His finger punched off the rifle's safety, but it was a handful of petitions. Robert spun to protect the fallen woman and saw Allen pitch forward with a bloody hole in the middle of his back. His hand went up to catch him, but a white-hot burning flew through his back and spurted a red ribbon from his chest. Robert thought he was falling, but he wasn't. He was rising into a blue infinity of indescribable happiness and knowing. All the beauty he had ever seen and all the joy he had ever felt more than ceased—they never were—in comparison to the place that he could see now hadn't been far away at all.

R obert. Robert—I love you."
    The sound of the words came as though slowly spinning to a stop with a soft cadence of their reality just beyond the darkness of his closed eyes. His hand was in hers, and he was on his back in a bed with his head elevated.

Robert opened his eyes to bright whiteness ebbing away from around her. She was crying without a sound, her brown eyes unblinking into his and welling over into two streams hesitating their way down her face. He wanted to tell her how beautiful she was, how the flecks of gold in her eyes were as bright as that day in the sun with Michael and Penny, but a heavy exhaustion hung stubbornly on to him from what must have been something awful.

"Daddy—Daddy!" Then Michael and Penny were holding on to him, and he was trying feebly to return their hugs as best he could with tubes fastened into his arms swinging and dangling. It was like that day in the kitchen when he had proposed and their heads were all together, and they were laughing and crying on the floor.

"I love you," Robert was whispering again and again into their hair and ears. "I love you, Penny . . . Michael . . . Beatrice . . . I love you."

Subdued cheering, clapping, and commotion sounded beyond them when a man's stern voice ordered, "You folks please stay back a minute! Mrs. Farr, Michael, Penny—please step back just a little, and don't get that close to his chest! This man is still in critical condition!"

Robert was released, and Beatrice and the children retreated a few steps as an intent, young-looking doctor with dark hair came to the side of the bed to check the tubes, a machine, and Robert. "How do you feel?" he asked, turning to the patient.

"Awfully . . . awfully tired," Robert managed.

"I should say!" the man replied. "I'm Doctor Uriah Bennett, a cardiologist here at Mount Kent Hospital in Washington, D.C. I've basically lived right here with you and your friend these past three days. You were brought in Friday, and this is Sunday. Do you remember what happened?"

"I . . . ," Robert started to answer unclearly, then it all surged back in sharp detail . . . Allen pitching forward with . . . Urgently, Robert asked, "How is Allen?"

Dr. Bennett answered, "Alive, stable, and conscious. Barring complications, both of you should have full but *slow* recoveries." He hesitated, then said in a lower tone of voice, "As a medical doctor, I feel constrained to tell you something. I've already told your family and these folks."

The doctor stepped back and gestured to two people just inside the door. Carol Mayhew-Barr came into focus as she took a step forward with a hopeful, teary smile. Robert held his hand out to her, and she came and squeezed it. "Robert, I've got so much to tell you," she whispered.

"And she will—later," Dr. Bennett said softly.

Pastor John came and stood beside her. "We prayed," he said simply. "Robert, we prayed." Carol and the pastor moved over to form a semicircle around the foot of the bed along with Beatrice, Michael, Penny, and Dr. Bennett.

The doctor again spoke softly. "What I want to say to you is this: Mr. Farr, we did everything humanly and technologically possible to save your life and Dr. Johnson's." The man paused as if to compose himself. "All of our technology . . . all of our efforts . . . fell far short of being enough. We knew that at every step. By every count, you and Allen Johnson should be dead—you should have died shortly after you were brought in."

Dr. Bennett cleared his throat. "Something most unusual happened." He glanced at the ceiling. "It was as if . . . I knew, and some of the nurses knew . . . and one of the doctors agrees—It was as if . . . Someone . . . came in about the time your vital functions should have ceased." He again cleared his throat. "I have to be honest. I have to say that we did every procedure indicated by your very severe condition—the bullet grazed your heart—Everything we did, we knew would not be enough, but—Mr. Farr, what I'm trying to say is that I believe the Highest Power took over your and Allen Johnson's cases. We went step-by-step knowing that what we were doing wasn't near enough, but we . . . we never even lost your heartbeat—or that of Dr. Johnson."

There was silence except for the clicking of a machine somewhere. "Since," said the doctor, "this has not been a routine situation, I allowed your family and these two friends to come here into CCU, as we saw indications that you might be coming around. They—well, we—got a little enthusiastic, as you might have heard."

"I heard," Robert whispered. "It helped."

"I'm asking them to leave now and return to the waiting area. There are some remarkable things they have to tell you, and they'll do that later after we check you again and you get some rest. Dr. Johnson is in the next room, on the other side of that wall. He said to tell you that the fishing trip is still on."

"The others," murmured Robert, "how are they?"

"A woman and a man were killed."

"The woman . . . was pregnant. How . . ."

"The baby was saved. It's a boy, and he's doing fine."

Robert felt tears release and trickle down his face.

"Everyone out," said Dr. Bennett, and they all reluctantly complied, especially Michael and Penny, who kept saying, "Daddy, I love you!" even when they were beyond the door.

For a moment, Robert was left alone. It had been three days. He tried to remember what had passed through his mind during that time, but his chest was hurting, and he would probably need something for pain. For the most part, all he could recall of the three days were fleeting impressions that didn't feel greatly new. There was a phrase that came to mind from a day that seemed a lifetime ago—and yet, that day was less than two months gone. But the expression had started it all, and now the same words described the last three days. *A moment of silence.* Robert closed his eyes in the little cubicle of a room, and even with the pain there was great peace. They were waiting for him.

A little more than an hour later, Dr. Bennett came back and announced that he was going home to get some sleep. The folks in the waiting room, he said, had provided him with a full account of all that had happened. At the very least. the doctor promised, he was going to read the Bible through He had never given the book much thought, but he was going to read it and investigate its claims. Aside from what he had seen firsthand from the medical perspective these last three days, Robert's family, pastor, and Carol were, well, they were special people, very special. "They'll be in," he said, "shortly." He looked at Robert for several heartbeats, then slowly turned and was gone.

A few minutes later, Beatrice, Michael, Penny, Pastor John, and Carol were standing around Robert's bed as a nurse was leaving the little room. The pastor said, "Robert, we're limited in the time we can stay. Dr. Bennett has been wonderful. Frankly, he's bent some rules. He said you should be up to this visit if we keep it short, then Beatrice can come back in four hours.

"When we got the word," the pastor continued, "of what happened on the steps of the Supreme Court, the church went to prayer. People came into the sanctuary as the word spread. We prayed around the clock. Our folks came as they could, stayed as they could—and prayed.

Duffy and a few others are still there. Mrs. Puckett is still there. Senator Tave Perrin flew down and prayed with us. Beatrice's parents drove her and Michael and Penny up as soon as word came of the shooting. Cyrus, Carol, and I got a flight into D.C. last night."

"Cyrus is here?" Robert asked weakly.

"Yes," Carol answered. "He's in the waiting room. With Senator Perrin." With that, Carol buried her face in her hands and wept. Beatrice moved around the children and put an arm around Carol's shoulders. That seemed to help, though both women were wiping their faces with tissues. Finally, Carol, pressing a wad of tissues against her eyes, brokenly said, "Robert—" With obvious effort, she took her hands down and looked at Robert with her eyes streaming and said, "When I heard . . .

"When I heard . . . about the shooting . . . Friday afternoon, I was at school. Cyrus called." Carol took a deep, labored breath. "I went . . . I went to the intercom . . ." Again, she broke down but then went on. "I said over the intercom—Robert, I said . . . all over the school . . . I said, 'Robert Farr has just been shot in Washington, D.C. I'm asking that we have a moment of silence . . . and that everyone pray for him.'

"Silently, in my heart and mind, Robert—I prayed for you, and I called on Jesus Christ to save me! After the silence, I said over the intercom—" Now through her tears, Carol was smiling, then she was laughing and wiping at her face with a little girl's excitement. "I broke the silence, Robert . . . for the whole school to hear . . . for all the world to hear! I prayed out loud with my finger dug into that intercom button, 'God, please have mercy on us! In the name of Jesus Christ . . . Amen.'"

Carol stood looking, still smiling as though at Someone unseen. She whispered, "I prayed. He was there and He heard."

Robert shut his eyes against his own flooding tears. He raised his hands and felt them there clutching his hands and embracing his arms. He opened his eyes into Beatrice's inches above his own. Right now, they didn't need to say the words. Wearily, Robert closed his eyes again. Then he realized it was Easter.

Aubrey Jones lives with his wife, Evelyn, and their two daughters in Kinston, North Carolina, where he is pastor of First Baptist Church. A graduate of both New Orleans Baptist Theological Seminary and Southern Baptist Theological Seminary, Aubrey has served as moderator of the Neuse Baptist Association. He has also been a member of the Board of Ministers at Campbell University and of the Cape Fear Literacy Council. *A Moment of Silence* is his first novel.